DC

Rain M̶e̶d̶d̶u̶s̶t̶a̶

Ireland 2010

Front Cover Photography by Mike Batty

ISBN - 13: 978-1456420130
ISBN – 10: 1456420135

This book is dedicated to Kit,

always constant.

CHAPTER 1

The Dog opened his eyes as the alarm rang out and wriggled happily up the bed towards his sleeping mistress. Tail thumping, he licked Hillary's face joyfully bringing her swiftly from the dream she was having, to the sunny bedroom.

'Good boy, Timber,' she said scratching the lurcher's ears affectionately. 'Happy Birthday to me.'

Hillary had been dreaming she was at school lining up to enter an examination hall to sit an exam she had forgotten to revise for. 'Damn,' she thought, 'am I ever going to quit having that dream?'

Timber stood up and marched bouncily on the spot, delighted it was walk time. Hillary climbed slowly out of bed and pulled a blue cotton jumper over her T-shirt and slipped in to her jeans. Walking slowly into the kitchen barefoot she ruffled the dog's head as he padded beside her. She filled the kettle and put it on, then sat on the kitchen floor to pull on socks and boots.

Clipping on Timber's lead she opened the cottage door and walked out into the fresh autumn morning. The sky was clear and cold, weak sunlight promising a beautiful day. Hillary opened the gate and paused to open her mailbox. The dog pulled, anxious to get going. Three cards lay in the box. The first in a bright yellow envelope bore her sister's familiar handwriting. The second she could see was from her old school friend Isabel. The third; this was the one she had been hoping for. The deep pink envelope she knew was from Nicky. Taking the cards indoors she opened just the one before resuming her walk.

For My Girlfriend on Her Birthday.

Hillary smiled, patted the dog again and went out.

*

Nicky lay in bed, her long dark hair fanning across the pillow. She had been awake for half an hour, the sun streaming through the window having awoken her. Today was Hillary's birthday. Nicky hoped the card had arrived on time. Nicky herself was thirty-eight. She had known Hillary for two months now and was completely in love. She opened her bedside drawer and pulled out a box of tissues. Feeling under the tissues she withdrew the photographs of Hillary that she had printed from her computer. Four colour snaps of Hillary sitting at her computer smiling coyly into the camera on top of her monitor. Her hair was glossy black, short at the back and sides with a long fringe framing her grey expressive eyes. Hillary looked very boyish and much younger than her thirty-six years. Her smile was open, innocent and slightly shy.

Nicky hoped that Dermot, Hillary's husband, had not reached the mailbox first in time to question the card with the English postmark. But no; Hillary was always incredibly careful. Nicky thought Hillary's life would be a lot less complicated if she had told Dermot about Nicky, simply introducing her as a friend. But Hillary wasn't coping well with the guilt she felt over their affair.

Of course, technically it wasn't an affair. Not really. They were two women who had fallen in love with one another on the internet and spent all their days talking either on the computer or on the phone. No crime had been committed. Was it possible to love someone you had never met?

She got up and made tea and toast, collected the paper and went back into bed.

*

Hillary and the dog walked contentedly towards the lake, their pace easy. Hillary thought she had never had a happier birthday. It was eleven months now since she had come out to herself. That date November 24th, 1997 was the biggest milestone in her life. The day she had stopped living a lie. It had been such a simple coming out, yet it had changed her life overnight. She had persuaded Dermot to take her to the pictures... one of the handful of times he had done so in their thirteen year marriage. The film had a lesbian character in the central role. And that, quite simply was all it took to make Hillary face up to the reason her marriage was celibate; to face up to the fact that she had been hiding something all her life... Something she knew to be a fact. That she was gay.

*

Nicky would have loved to phone Hillary right there and then to wish her a happy birthday but there were two reasons why this wasn't possible. One was that fact that Hillary made her promise never to phone either her home phone or mobile without a text from Hillary first to say the coast was clear. Secondly, today was a Friday and Hillary thought Nicky worked in an office on Thursdays and Fridays. So the call would have to wait until tonight when Dermot did what he did every evening, which was to go straight from work to the pub.

Nicky finished her breakfast, showered, dressed and strolled out into the sun towards her *Jeep* to begin her day.

*

Hillary's life had begun to change slowly following her life-changing cinema outing. She cut her hair shorter and began to allow herself to begin to read lesbian magazines and books. She had always been a quiet introverted woman but now her life became more secretive. The lesbian literature was hidden in the attic, like some kind of contraband. She had been a housewife for most of her married life, occasionally taking the odd part time job, but never keeping them because Hillary had another secret. She was socially painfully shy to the extent that she suffered panic attacks. It was easier to hide here at home tending to her beloved garden. Much later in her life she was to realise just how much keeping her gayness a secret, even from herself, had affected her socially.

Hillary eased herself into her new life as a lesbian slowly, like someone breaking in new shoes. She identified with the women in the gay magazines and found comfort in the knowledge that many women like her had come out late in life. Hillary was leading a sad life with her husband who was both a bully and a drunk. But up until now she had had no idea how to change it. She had no desire to try to find another man, and she neither had the life skills nor the desire to live alone. She had been content up until now to tend her beloved garden and to join Dermot in the pub the odd time she desired company. But the pubs Dermot drank in were mainly frequented by men, farmers mostly, for Hillary lived in rural Ireland and she did not have any women friends. Her friendships with women were at best awkward. She now knew this was because she required a deeper level of intimacy than was normally the case. Hillary was an incredibly romantic person and casual friendships did not fulfil her. She yearned to be loved, more than anything. However since that fateful day in November she knew she was capable of turning her life around completely. Once she was fully accepting of herself as a lesbian she was determined to find a girlfriend. Love was now a possibility once again in her life, something she had not believed since finding her marriage such a disappointment all those years ago.

Hillary did not rush things. She waited eight months, gradually feeling her way into her new skin before she took the next step. The next step was to come out to someone. And that someone would be Peter.

Peter had been Hillary's best friend since they were nineteen, back when they played in the same band together, when Hillary had lived in England. Peter had visited Hillary in Ireland faithfully every year since she had moved away to get married. Visits which Dermot had tolerated grudgingly. But Peter had bored of visiting the same village every year and wanted to see more of Ireland. Dermot was peculiar in the fact that he was so unadventurous he never wanted to go away on holiday, having taken Hillary on just one holiday in the whole time they were together. Peter had tried to persuade Hillary to accompany him on a trip and leave Dermot behind if he didn't want to go, but up until now she had not dared.

But now, with growing confidence she decided she would plan a holiday with Peter, as part of her new found independence, and on that holiday Peter would be the first person she came out to.

The holiday, to Ballybay on the southwest coast had been a great success. Hillary had left a note on the kitchen table for Dermot: "Gone on holiday, back in eight days" and was able to put the idea of facing his wrath to the back of her mind, for going on holiday without his permission.

She told Peter she was gay on the first night as they had drinks after dinner. His reaction was one of delight... mainly because he had been advising her to leave Dermot for years and now saw, as Hillary did, that this would inevitably follow. Peter had not seen it coming but he said an awful lot of things now fell into place. It was a revelation full of good-hearted teasing, especially when Hillary confessed to having had a crush on Peter's first girlfriend.

Peter and Hillary had sat contentedly on the sea wall in Ballybay and watched all kinds of women walk by, while Peter quizzed her about which ones she fancied, congratulating her on the feminine ones and admonishing her for the butch ones. Hillary was not nearly brave enough to approach any women, realising that to chat up a woman who may not, after all, be gay was a risky business. But all the same she made a vow to Peter that day.

'I'm going to find a woman to love' she had said, 'and I'm going to bring her back here to Ballybay for a romantic holiday.' It was a promise she somehow knew she would keep.

'But how on earth are you going to meet gay women living where you live?' Peter had asked, 'It's rare a straight woman goes into that awful pub in your village, never mind a gay one.'

But Hillary knew the answer to that one.

'The internet.' she replied.

*

It both helped and didn't help that Dermot was a computer expert. In fact his business was computer consultancy. Hillary had heard you could chat to other people from around the world on the internet, but in Ireland in August 1998, the system was very much in its infancy. Dermot was very dubious when Hillary said she wanted to try "chat", saying that everyone on it would be weirdoes and men pretending to be women. But Hillary was adamant; she felt it would be a way to make new friends. So he helped her find a way into a chat room. The rest was up to her, i.e. the business of finding her way into a lesbian chat room without leaving a trail that Dermot could follow.

She managed to convince Dermot to get her a book about the internet and studied it diligently. It was difficult to follow, but the dream of connecting with other lesbians spurred her along. She had found a gay chat room but every time she tried to enter, the computer would crash. It was so frustrating because she could not ask Dermot for help. Even if he did not guess her reasons for wanting to enter it, he was terribly homophobic and would forbid her from talking to 'queers'.

Eventually, one night when Dermot was working away from home overnight, just when she was close to giving up, Hillary got into the chat room. With a mixture of joy and fear she saw there were two women in there, Corgi and Topcat. Her first contact with other gay women. Giving herself the name "Dove" she slowly typed,

'Hello.'

Corgi was in Australia. They were talking about a balloonist who had ditched in the sea off Australia. Hillary joined in, her heart beating fast at the thrill of being with women like herself at last. Corgi was typing at work and had to leave when her boss came in. Hillary was alone with Topcat.

'Where are you from, Topcat?'

'London... How about you?'

'Ireland.'

'I like Irish accents.'

And so it began.

At first Hillary was afraid to say she was married in case she was ridiculed and chased out of the room. But Topcat told her how to download a messenger service, which was a means of chatting in private.

The first thing Hillary said was,

'My name is Hillary. I'm married.'

'Nice to meet you Hillary, I'm Nicky.'

Hillary knew somehow, deep inside, she had found the love of her life. They got on like a house on fire and very soon exchanged photos, after Nicky explained how to add them as attachments to e-mails. Nicky was both handsome and beautiful at the same time, olive skinned with dark chocolate brown eyes and a beautiful smile.

The past two months had flown by. They would talk every night on the computer while Dermot was at the pub. Hillary told Nicky the story of her life, and much more too, her hopes and fears; her dreams. Nicky was a great listener but needed to be coaxed to talk about herself. She lived alone and seemed to live a very quiet life. Both Nicky and Hillary often sat drinking together, one in Ireland, one in England talking into the small hours. When Dermot's *Land Rover* pulled up Hillary would type "D" and quickly turn off the computer and race into bed. Dermot usually came home about 2.30am and Hillary didn't like talking to him when he was so drunk. In fact she was finding it hard to talk to him at all these days. All she thought about was Nicky, beautiful Nicky.

Friday nights were Hillary's favourite nights to chat but at the weekends she was always left wanting, having to chat to her other computer friends. Nicky worked in the offices of a big hardware store on Thursdays and Fridays and by Friday nights she was too tired to do anything except sleep. On Saturday and Sunday nights she liked to go for a drink, or would often spend the entire weekends with her sister in Bath with whom she was very close. When Hillary asked her who she spent the time with, Nicky said that she just talked to the barman.

Hillary had noticed that Nicky didn't talk about herself much and was often vague about many things. But Hillary was too in love to care. She would have liked to have asked Nicky to spend weekend nights with her occasionally but didn't feel she had the right to ask. She had her company all through the week and that was enough.

CHAPTER 2

Hillary and Timber walked slowly back to the house, woman and dog enjoying the beautiful October morning. Hillary opened the birthday cards from her sister and Isabel and placed them on the mantelpiece, then opened the one from Dermot that was lying on the table along with a wrapped box of *After Eight* mints.

To My Wife on Her Birthday
She put it with the others. She looked at Nicky's card again and tucked it inside the pages of a book. There was no card from Peter, he always forgot and rang her a few days later.

She walked through the large sunny garden, down the little path that led to the shed. Taking a fork and spade down from the hooks on the wall she went to where she was making a new vegetable patch and set the spade and fork into the ground.

Returning to the house she took her radio from the kitchen and brought it down to where she was about to work. She set it on an upturned bucket to protect it from the dewy grass. She turned it on and tuned into *BBC Radio Four* and began turning the earth.

As she worked she thought about how much she wanted to meet Nicky. She herself was more than ready but Nicky had not mentioned this yet. It was a well-known cliché that lesbians tended to rush into relationships. Where do lesbians go on their second date? The estate agents.

Was she rushing things, feeling it was now time to meet? Surely two months was long enough? She looked up over her spade and imagined how it would feel to see Nicky driving up the lane towards her. She was thirty-six – no longer a young woman. She was sure when she met Nicky her feelings would only grow stronger. She would mention it tonight she decided; take the birthday girl's prerogative, when Nicky phoned.

Dermot popped home from work before going to the pub as a special concession to her birthday. She had already told him she wanted to spend her birthday evening watching a video, and he had brought the one she asked for from town. He did not express surprise at this, except to say, "Are you sure you don't want to come to the pub?" He was used to her staying in all the time.

The minute Dermot drove off to the pub she went outside to close the five-barred gate behind him. He always asked her to leave it open for him but she used the excuse that it made her feel safer with it shut while he was out. In fact it was a ruse to give her time to shut the computer down, or put the phone back and compose herself if he came home while she was talking to Nicky.

She took the phone from its base and laid it beside her on the couch, then opened a can of lager. She put more logs on the fire and dimmed the lights. Putting the video in the recorder she wound it forward to approximately the middle and left the remote control on the table next to her beer. If Dermot came back unexpectedly she would be in the middle of watching the video. Then she wrote her text to Nicky:

Coast is clear, ready for your call

The call never came. After half an hour Hillary sent the text again. After an hour she rewound the video and started watching it.

*

It was 11pm. Hillary had watched the film and drank three of the four lagers from the fridge. She drifted onto the computer and logged on. She signed onto the messenger service. No Topcat. She went into the chat room. A young woman she knew, a student from Bristol with the nickname Fluffy was in the room.

'Hi Dove," she typed. 'Happy birthday.'

'Thanks. Have you seen Topcat tonight?'

'No but I was looking for her myself. You two lovebirds not on the phone tonight?'

'I was expecting a call but she hasn't phoned. What were you looking for her for?'

'I am going up to London next weekend. I was hoping she'd meet me and show me round some of the gay bars.'

'That sounds like fun. If I see her I'll mention it.'

'Why don't you come over yourself, Dove, and join us?'

'D would never allow it... besides I'd get panicky in a big city like London.'

'When is she coming over to Ireland to see you?'

'I don't know. Soon I hope. I'm off to bed now. Talk to you soon.'

Hillary logged off the computer, put the phone back, kissed the dog on the top of his head and went to bed.

*

Nicky did not appear for the rest of the weekend. Hillary drifted around in a daze feeling sad and confused. Dermot worked this weekend as usual so at least she didn't have to try to make small talk. On Monday afternoon Hillary checked her e-mail. There was one there from Nicky sent an hour earlier.

Hi Babe,
> *So sorry I didn't get to phone you on your birthday. My nephew Dean was taken ill on Friday afternoon. He was taken to hospital and has been diagnosed with severe anaemia. I had to drive over there and look after the horses while my sister and Bob stayed with Dean in the hospital. In my rush down there I forgot my mobile phone, and didn't want to phone you without prior arrangement in case D was there. I've just got back and am shattered so don't know if I'll be online tonight. Miss you like crazy and hope you managed to have a nice birthday anyway,*
> *Loads of Love,*
> *Nicky x x x*

A flood of relief and guilt swept over Hillary. She had been selfish only thinking of herself all weekend. It never occurred to her that Nicky might have troubles of her own. She e-mailed back, wishing the little boy a

18

speedy recovery and telling Nicky not to worry about coming onto the computer tonight if she was tired.

Hillary knew her need to speak to Nicky everyday was slightly obsessional but living this way, loving a woman without ever being able to hold her was horrible. Hillary told herself to get busy in the house for the rest of the day. She never rang Nicky herself because she didn't want Nicky's phone number on her bill; something Dermot would most certainly quiz her about, and Nicky hadn't suggested phoning today, so she would just have to be patient. It was time she gave her cupboards a good clean out.

*

Autumn turned to winter. Hillary lived for her talks with Nicky during the week. She now went out less and less. During weekends she moped around, aware her life was drifting by and she was no closer to doing what she wanted to do which was to meet Nicky.

As the weeks past Hillary learned Nicky's upbringing had been very different from her own. Born to a Polish mother and English father, Nicky and her sister, Imogen, had attended private schools run by nuns. The girls' father had made of lot of money and they enjoyed the luxury of having a large swimming pool in their garden. Nicky's parents were sociable and did a lot of entertaining. They were full of fun, even maintaining a positive outlook when Nicky's father lost most of his money and the big house and swimming pool had to go. Nicky's upbringing sounded a world apart form Hillary's who had lived on a council estate.

In spite of all this the two women had a lot in common. Being only two years apart in age they reminisced about music and films of the same era. They shared a similar sense of humour. They had even both lost their parents in the same years. Both had one older sister, but Nicky told Hillary that Imogen strongly disapproved of Nicky's lesbianism. This was to make life difficult.

It was now Christmas Eve and Nicky and Hillary were on messenger saying their goodbyes. Nicky was about to drive down to Bath, to spend two weeks with Imogen and Bob and their two children. Imogen didn't have a computer and Nicky hinted it might be difficult to ring from her sister's house.

Hillary typed,

But aren't you entitled to a life of your own?

and then deleted it before pressing send. Hillary had noticed Nicky seemed to tiptoe around her sister, due to Imogen's views on lesbianism. Nicky often was unable to phone Hillary because Imogen was visiting. She had said that Imogen knew of the relationship but found it very distasteful, so the two never discussed it. Hillary thought this was very wrong but it always seemed to upset Nicky if she said anything about it. The two women said their goodbyes and as Hillary half expected, Nicky allowed the whole two weeks to pass without getting in touch.

*

In the March of the New Year something wonderful happened. Dermot announced he was going on a fishing trip down to Kerry with some of his friends.

Straight away Hillary had the thought that this was her big chance to meet Nicky. That night Hillary rushed onto the computer with her news.

'He's leaving on Friday and will be away till the Saturday of the next week,' she gushed.

'Will you come over and see me?'

'Oh babe, I'd love to, but I have to work all of that week doing overtime for stocktaking.'

Hillary was quashed. She had been certain Nicky was going to say yes. She tried not to feel bitter about the fact that Nicky had actually taken time off work to meet the student from the chat room who had travelled up to London for a visit.

Hillary spent the week alone. Nicky wasn't even available much to talk to on the phone or computer because she was so tired after working extra hours. On the Friday before Dermot came back, Nicky surprised Hillary by phoning her at five o'clock in the evening.

'Hello Nicky. What a lovely surprise! Shouldn't you be at work?'

'I got off early to ring you. I'm going out tonight with Linda and some of the gang so it's my only chance to talk to you.'

'That's nice. I hope you have a great time.'

Later that night Hillary rang her old school friend Isabel.

'I hate to admit to this but I'm starting to have doubts about Nicky.'

'What do you mean, what's wrong?'

'I'm starting to wonder if she's seeing someone else. I don't think she's serious about meeting me.'

'Well then you shouldn't waste anymore time," said Isabel. 'Confront her and see what she says.'

Hillary hugged the dog close to her and wept. She was afraid that if she confronted Nicky it would be all over. But Isabel was right. She couldn't waste any more time. Settling herself down in front of the computer she dried her tears and began to write the e-mail she knew she should have written a long time ago.

Dear Nicky,
       I hope you had a nice night out with Linda and the gang. I don't know how to say this nicely so I'm just going to say it. Are you really serious about ever meeting me? You must know that this is a serious relationship to me, and that I hope one day we will live together. Seven months have gone by and you still have no plans to meet me. I've tried to be patient. Is it time I gave up?
      All my love as ever, Hillary x x x

*

The next day was Saturday; the day Dermot was due back. Hillary lay in bed with no real desire to get up. The dog seemed to sense her mood and lay still at the foot of the bed. Outside rain fell steadily and very heavily.

The trouble was, it had been so long since Hillary had 'dated' anyone that she was unable to judge whether her attitude was reasonable or not. She had rather meekly challenged Nicky once before about going out so much at the weekends and not making more time available to talk to her. Nicky had replied rather stiffly that it was unhealthy for them to spend every night of the week tapping away talking to each other and had said she only wished Hillary would go out more. Even though she didn't like Dermot's company she would be out and about amongst people and might even make some new friends. Hillary knew this answer made sense yet it still left her with an uneasy feeling that Nicky was somehow keeping her at arms length.

Hillary snuggled deeper into the duvet. Now she had thought it over, she half-regretted sending Nicky that e-mail. She tried to run over exactly what she had said in the short letter. She hated coming across as being clingy and yet she knew she couldn't go on the way she was. With a heavy sigh she climbed out of bed and went to check her e-mail.

Friday night/ Saturday morning 2.30am
Dear Hillary,
I got in from the pub a couple of hours ago but couldn't sleep so logged on to see if you were around. I wont be around tomorrow as I'm driving into town to see about buying another car and part exchanging this one .I also need to see about getting another job as I need to raise my income. I hope if D comes back early he is in a good mood and not nasty to you.
Thanks for the e-mail. You must know that I love you very much and I know we will meet some day. I'm short of cash at the moment but we will get to see your beloved Ballybay together, I promise.
Hope you are snuggled up and having pleasant dreams.
Thinking of you my sweet Dove,
All my love, Nicky x x x

Hillary read it over three times. It sounded reasonable but Nicky was still vague about meeting. "Some day" she had said. Somehow that didn't feel like some day soon.

CHAPTER 3

It was now summer. Hillary took Timber for longer and longer walks and also started a keep fit regime, doing a hundred sit-ups and a hundred push-ups every morning. She even started doing lifts with a twenty pound crow bar that she had found in the garage. She wanted to make sure she was looking the best she could when she met Nicky. She worked every day in the garden. It was almost an acre and mowing it all alone could pass a full day.

Her relationship with Dermot was one of two strangers who occasionally passed each other in the house. She would time her walk with Timber to coincide with Dermot taking his shower and leaving the house. The majority of the time she would come back to find his *Land Rover* gone and him off to work. The next she would hear of him was his car returning from the pub around 2.20am – the cue for her to dash into bed from the computer or phone. She would hear him drunkenly talking to the dog through the wall; his monotone heavily laced with swearwords, usually an indictment of the men he had just been drinking with.

It was months now since Hillary had been out with him. She found it totally embarrassing being in his company when he was so inebriated, even though most of his mates would be in the same state. But his drunkenness did have one advantage. Dermot would leave his trousers on the bedroom floor before getting into bed; his pockets stuffed with notes and coins.

Hillary had to ask Dermot for every penny and explain what she wanted it for. He would then hand her the money in a proud lordly manner, which Hillary hated. It was for this reason that Hillary had no qualms in helping herself to a handful of pound coins every night and sometimes even notes if he had a lot of cash on him. By the simple method of taking a small amount every night she had accrued nearly a thousand pounds. This was stashed in the attic along with the lesbian literature and a new outfit she had bought at Christmas. The things for her new life. Hillary was delighted with the sum because this was enough to pay for a week in the beautiful old hotel that she and Peter had stayed at in Ballybay. Nicky's money worries need now not be part of the equation.

It was a Friday evening in June and Hillary was working in the garden. Nicky normally got home from work around six-thirty but she would only spend half an hour on the computer talking to Hillary because at seven Nicky always went out to buy food. Nicky was the only person Hillary had heard of who never kept any food in the house.

Hillary was particularly happy this evening because she had made a decision to surprise Nicky with a phone call. If Dermot noticed the London number on the phone bill she would say it was the number of Anne, an old school friend whom she'd recently got back in touch with. It was in fact true she had recently got back in touch with Anne, but they had corresponded by letter and not by phone.

At a quarter to seven Hillary brought the phone down to a leafy bower at the bottom of the big garden. It was a favourite place to sit. She felt relaxed and happy. She was going to ask Nicky directly to come with her to Ballybay and she had even set a date for it ... July the fourteenth. She had decided her problem was that she had not been specific about meeting Nicky and that it was high time one of them set a date. Smiling to herself she dialled Nicky's number.

'Hello?'

A man's voice answered.

Completely thrown, Hillary stammered, 'Hello, is Nicky there please?'

'Just a minute, I'll get her.'

A few seconds later Nicky's voice came on the line.

'Hello Nicky, its Hillary.'

'Hillary! What a surprise.'

'Who was that who just answered the phone?'

'Oh, that was Jack, my new lodger.'

'Lodger?'

'Yes I've found an answer to my financial problems. I'm renting out one of my spare bedrooms to him for fifty quid a week. He's just moving his stuff in tonight.'

'Wow! And you don't mind having a stranger in the house?'

'Jack's an old friend of the family. I ran into him last week and he needed a place nearer work and I needed some money so we came to an arrangement.'

'What does he do?'

'Financial stuff. He works in the city.'

'Oh.' Hillary knew her voice sounded flat but she couldn't hide it. A new lodger meant that Nicky intended to be single for quite some time. Somehow it meant there was even less room in Nicky's life for Hillary.

'He's got his own bathroom,' Nicky said filling the silence. 'I probably won't see that much of him.'

'That's great news,' said Hillary unable to hide the disappointment in her voice. She felt stupid being jealous of a lodger but it was just one more person who seemed to have an access to Nicky that Hillary didn't.

'I've got to go back out in a minute. I'm helping him move his stuff over. It's going to take several trips,' said Nicky. 'Was there a special reason you phoned? What will you say if Dermot asks you about this number on your bill?'

'I'll say it's Anne's.'

Hillary felt so deflated she no longer felt like mentioning the holiday. What rotten luck that the first time she rang Nicky she was in the middle of something. But she'd started so she'd better finish.

'Well actually I'm phoning to officially invite you to go on holiday with me to Ballybay. I've saved up a grand so I'll have enough to pay for all the accommodation. I thought July the fourteenth would be a good time to go. All you will have to bring is yourself and some spending money.'

'Bastille Day, huh?' said Nicky. 'Well of course I'd love to go if I can fit it in with work. I'll let you know as soon as I can. I'd better go now. Got to try and get all Jack's stuff moved in before dark.'

'Okay. I won't keep you. Will you be on the computer later on?'

'I'm not sure. Jack might want to go for a drink later. If I get on it'll be late. Okay?'

'Alright, bye Nicky.'

'Bye for now.'

Hillary switched the phone off with a heavy sigh and looked at the dog beside her.

'Well that sure didn't go how I planned, Timber.'

She was no nearer meeting Nicky, who had sounded very non-committal. Plus now she had someone else to be jealous of along with Imogen the sister, Linda the friend, all the gang from Nicky's local, and now Jack the lodger. But Hillary knew it wasn't just jealousy of Nicky's friends that was bothering her. It was the sense that Nicky's life progressed happily on its way without any indication there might be someday room for Hillary.

Nicky did not appear on the computer that night. Hillary hadn't really expected her to and went to bed with a heavy heart. But there was an e-mail the next day, as usual written in the wee small hours:

Dear Hillary,

Sorry I was a bit flustered when you rang, there were just boxes everywhere and it had to be all sorted out before dark. I would love to go to Ballybay with you on July 14ᵗʰ. I'm sure it will be all right with work. I'm dragging Jack to a used car auction tomorrow as I still want to change the car and he knows something about them. Might see you on the computer on Sunday. I'm very excited about Ballybay now, Love you heaps, Nicky x x x

*

It was Friday, July the tenth. The weather was gorgeously hot. Hillary sat in her garden soaking up the rays. Unbelievably she was going to meet Nicky in four days time. She felt very happy and excited. Her bags had been packed weeks ago, and sat in the attic. Suddenly Hillary noticed she could hear a strange buzzing sound. A sound that was coming and going. It was too loud to be an insect. Hillary realised it was coming from overhead. With a sense of horror she looked up and saw that there was steam coming from the tips of the big pine trees that surrounded the big garden. As she gazed, there was another buzzing sound and a little lick of flame rose from the treetop.

'Oh shit!' she shouted scrambling to her feet. The wet treetops were touching the overhead power lines that passed by the house to the pole in the garden. Sprinting across the garden she imagined one of the live wires burning through and falling onto her as she ran.

Once inside the house she grabbed the telephone with shaking hands and dialled Dermot's number.

'Dermot the trees in the garden are on fire. They're touching the power lines!'

'Well what do you expect me to do about it, I'm in a meeting.'

'You'll have to come home and call the electric company straight away.' Hillary ran outside still holding the phone. A gentle breeze was blowing the flames across the treetops so that now several of them were alight.

'Oh God! There's a row of flames along the tops now. The wind is blowing it all towards the house!'

'Hillary I've just told you I'm in a meeting.'

'Dermot, the house will catch fire! I'm frightened.'

'It will probably go out in a minute.'

Hillary began to sob. She was really scared now.

'Please, please! You've got to come.'

'Hillary, flames burn upwards, not down'

'Please!'

'Oh you stupid bitch! Now I have to leave this meeting all because you are frightened of a few sparks.' Dermot put the phone down. Hillary only cared that help was coming. Dermot's office was only six miles away.

When Dermot's car pulled into the drive all the flames were out.

'What the hell were you making such a fuss about?' he said looking at the trees.

Then under his breath, 'Christ, those power lines shouldn't be that low.'

As they stood on the drive there were several more buzzes and flashes and the whole row of treetops were alight again, the flames licking towards the bottom of the roof.

Dermot phoned the electric company. The electricity board worker was laconic about the sight that met him.

'The whole row of them needs topping. I'll put you down for an emergency topping early next week.'

'What if one of those wires burns through? What do I do if I have a live wire flailing round the garden?'

'Oh it'll probably short circuit out.'

'Probably!' Hillary was almost speechless.

'And if the house catches fire in the meantime who do I call first? The fire brigade or you?'

'Probably the fire brigade,' replied the man, completely missing the anger and irony in Hillary's voice.

The man drove away and Dermot went back to work. Hillary stayed indoors for the rest of the day and tried not to look out of the window. It was several hours before she realised this whole tree-topping operation might take place on Tuesday, the very day Nicky would be picking her up for their holiday.

The plan was that Nicky was to fly over from London to Dublin, pick up a hire car in Dublin and drive over to pick up Hillary. The estimated time of arrival was two o'clock. Then the two of them would drive down to Ballybay together.

Hillary wrote Nicky an anxious e-mail explaining about the whole tree disaster and telling Nicky to make sure Dermot's car was outside his office before coming to the house. Hillary was a born worrier and remained in a state about everything all weekend. It did not help that Nicky neither answered the e-mail nor appeared online all weekend. Hillary eventually rang Nicky's house on Sunday night only to find the line permanently engaged.

On Monday morning two lumberjacks arrived with big chainsaws. The first thing they asked Hillary was did she have a ladder. Hillary was incredulous that they had arrived without one. Luckily she had two very long ones and they set to work. Dermot had left Hillary with strict instructions that they were not to take too much off the trees and leave them "looking a sight". He refused to stay and supervise them himself even for a little while. He had another meeting. Hillary indicated the height which she wished the trees to be reduced to. The two men said that they would do their best but they had to work fast as the power was only going to be off for four hours. Hillary could see this was a near impossible task.

The mess was incredible. The whole garden was covered in large branches and the shape of what remained of the trees was ugly. Hillary knew the men had done their best and that the job had had to be done. She also knew that the trees would grow back in no time, making a thicker and more attractive barrier than was there before. However she knew Dermot would not see things this way. The men left and Hillary knew there was no point in her starting to clear up the mess until she got back from her holiday. She almost shook when she imagined what Dermot's reaction would be to the devastation in their garden. Fortunately he went straight to the pub from work without first coming home to check on the work. Dermot was what Hillary called a "blame merchant" and Hillary knew that while the electric company would be getting some of the blame, she would bear the brunt of most of it for not supervising the work properly. It would be dark when Dermot returned home so she had another day's grace before the inevitable explosion of rage occurred.

Life wasn't being kind to her, but nothing, absolutely nothing was going to stop her enjoying this holiday. She logged onto the computer, hoping to see Topcat come up on her list of chatters present. There was no Topcat but there was an e-mail.

Monday evening,
Hi Sweetheart,
Sorry I have been offline all weekend. Some workman digging a hole outside

my house cut off my electricity supply. What a time for it to happen, eh? I'm just dashing over to Linda's house to iron my holiday clothes. Sorry to hear about your tree trouble, glad no one was hurt. I will make sure D's car is at the office before I pick you up. If he's at home I'll just drive around till he's gone. Can't wait to see you,

All my love, Nicky x x x

*

On Tuesday morning Hillary woke up full of mixed emotions. Pure joy that today at last, after knowing her for eleven months she was finally going to meet Nicky. And fear of how Dermot was going to react when he saw his garden surrounded by ugly stubby trees. She slipped into her clothes and set off with an equally happy Timber towards the lake. It was a truly glorious morning. The sky was a clear blue and the sun was already high in the sky... not a cloud in sight.

*

Dermot was standing outside the back door when Hillary returned. As she had expected, his face was bright red with anger.

'You've allowed them to ruin our lovely garden,' he raged. His anger was no less frightening because she had known it was coming. She unclipped Timber's lead and tried to remain calm. Suddenly he grabbed the front of her sweatshirt and twisted it.

'Look at it! Just look at it!' he shouted dragging her back outside. He bent down to pick up a branch.

Hillary saw her chance and took it. She shook herself free and ran. Across the garden, through the gate and down the lane she ran. Veering into the woods she swerved between the trees until she was well hidden.

She had known Dermot would not follow her. He was so unfit he never walked anywhere never mind running. She knew he would storm off to his office and work up his rage anew in the pub that night, planning to take it out on her when he got home. He often did this when he was angry with her. She imagined he enjoyed thinking of her sweating out the hours until his return. But Hillary would not be there when Dermot got home. She would be in Ballybay with Nicky.

CHAPTER 4

Hillary crept home half an hour later, and as expected Dermot's car was gone. She got the ladder and went up into the attic and fetched down her bags. She carried them out to the front of the house and put them behind a tree. Then she went in and had a long bath and dressed in a white T-shirt, khaki combats and a red checked shirt. It was now eleven o'clock. She spent the next three hours sitting in the garden reading. At five past two her mobile phone rang. It was Nicky.

'Hi, I've just passed the office and Dermot's car is outside. I'll be with you in five minutes.'

Hillary flushed with excitement. She raced inside, said goodbye to Timber, who unfortunately wouldn't be getting a walk for a week, and locked the door. Now she was standing outside her front wall with her luggage hidden behind the tree. She heard a car coming and bent down pretending to be pulling weeds. In the very unlikely event of one of Dermot's friends or colleagues driving past she didn't want to be seen standing with rucksacks in her hand. She was being overcautious, she knew, but after waiting all this time, she was determined nothing was going to go wrong. The car passed. She had told Nicky what she would be wearing and that she would be standing on the roadside, as none of the houses in Hillary's road had numbers. She realised suddenly that she did not know what kind of car Nicky had hired or the colour. She heard another engine and instinctively knew this was Nicky. She bent down to tug on a weed and squinted up to see the driver. It was Nicky, looking just like her photo, smiling broadly driving towards her. She grabbed her bags and the second Nicky stopped she was in the back of the car and they were off again.

Her first impression had been that it looked like Nicky was sitting on the floor; the driver's seat was so low. They were in fact in a tiny car, and the impression was caused by her being used to Dermot's *Land Rover*. Hillary's first words to Nicky were something like 'Okay. Drive!' and she pulled the white baseball cap out of the top of her rucksack and rammed it low on her head covering her eyes. Even at this stage she half expected Dermot to be standing in the middle of the road just around the next bend with his hand raised.

'So!' said Nicky beaming into the rear view mirror at Hillary. 'How are you?'

'I'm fine. Dermot went mad about the trees. I had to run and hide in the woods till he'd gone.'

'Oh God, he didn't hurt you did he?'

'No, I'm fine,' replied Hillary. 'How was your flight?'

'Not nice. I'm not keen on flying,' said Nicky.

'Really? I wouldn't have guessed that.'

There was a long pause, while Nicky negotiated the twists and turns of the narrow lanes surrounding Hillary's house. Both women felt a little tongue-tied. In no time at all they were passing Dermot's office. Hillary had grabbed an atlas that lay on the back seat and covered her face with it.

'It's okay,' she heard Nicky say from over the top of the seat. 'His car's still there.'

37

Just after they passed Dermot's office Hillary put the map down, removed her cap and climbed over the front passenger seat and settled into it, putting on her seatbelt straight away. Nicky laughed with delight.

'I would have pulled over you know and let you in the front the normal way!'

'Ah well, I'm here now,' Hillary said in her soft Irish lilt and both women shyly glanced at each other for the first time.

It was lovely driving through the Irish countryside together. Hillary took off her shirt and sat in her white T-shirt with the window rolled down. Nicky sneaked glances at her biceps and her brown arms. Hillary was wearing sunglasses and was able to admire Nicky's long legs out of the corner of her eye without appearing to stare. They couldn't have wished for a more beautiful sunny day. Hillary had made a compilation CD of her favourite songs and sent it to Nicky at Christmas and Nicky had it playing now. The two women sang along and delighted in the feeling of being so close together.

'Poor old Timber won't be getting his walks this week,' said Hillary.

'He'll be okay,' said Nicky. 'Would you mind opening me the packet of cigarettes in the glove compartment there?' Hillary opened the cigarettes and lit one for Nicky. As she passed it over to Nicky, Nicky held on to her hand for a moment and both women felt the thrill of electricity pass between them.

Presently they stopped for a break. They were almost a third of the way to Ballybay now. Hillary had spotted a very old fashioned looking pub.

'It's time for you to experience your first Irish pub, Nicky,' said Hillary, and they went in. The interior seemed dark after the sunshine outside and the furnishings were scruffy. There was a musty smell. They sat at a little table after ordering a pot of tea and two cheese sandwiches. Hillary was sitting with her back to the window with the sun streaming in around her. Nicky sat opposite her. The two women looked at each other face to face for the first time.

Hillary was surprised at how shy she felt. Nicky was smaller and slimmer than she had imagined. She had a beautiful smile that lit up her face.

'You look lovely,' said Hillary, seriously.

'So do you,' said Nicky. They grinned at each other.

'I can't stop smiling,' said Hillary.

'Me neither. I hope we never do.'

They made one more stop, in a little café where they had chips and egg. In no time at all it was seven o' clock and they were descending the long hill into Ballybay.

Suddenly Nicky stopped the car and put the handbrake on. In silence she took her hands off the wheel, opened the driver's door and slid out of the car. As Nicky stood in the road Hillary thought 'Oh God! She's changed her mind! She doesn't want to go through with it.'

Hillary leaned over and in a frightened voice said, 'What is it Nicky? What's wrong?'

'Bee,' said Nicky. 'On the dash there.'

'Oh thank God!' exclaimed Hillary. 'I thought you were having second thoughts.'

Hillary scooped up the bee with the corner of the map and let it out of the car.

'My hero!' laughed Nicky, and climbed back in.

They descended the hill into the little fishing town.

'Oh Hillary it's gorgeous!' said Nicky. The streets thronged with tourists in gaily-coloured holiday clothes.

'It's so much busier than I imagined. I thought you'd pick a really quiet place.'

'The tourists are part of its charm.'

They drove around to the entrance to the hotel. Parking outside the front doors Nicky went in and asked how to access the car park. They had to circle the town twice before they found the narrow entrance. Hillary put her shirt back on and the two of them carried their luggage across the car park and into the foyer of the hotel. The carpet was a rich red and the antique furniture dark and deeply polished.

'What do you think of the hotel?' asked Hillary. 'Did I tell you its over three hundred years old?'

'It's perfect, Hillary. Just perfect.'

'I'm glad you like it. I think it's just the right size. Not so small that you feel under scrutiny, but not big and impersonal either.'

They checked in and carried their luggage up to the room, which was large and elaborately furnished.

'What a lovely room,' said Nicky. 'You are so clever to have found this place. And now, do you know what its time for? A big pint of *Guinness*!'

'You deserve it,' Hillary smiled. Well done driving us here. You must be exhausted especially having come all the way from Dublin in the first place.'

'I hope I don't have to sit in that car again for a very long time. Come on, let's hit the bar!'

*

Hillary and Nicky sat opposite each other in a little booth near the bar. Hillary stretched and took a long drink of her ice-cold lager.

'I can't believe we're really here at last. Can you?'

'Oh it's just fantastic, babe. I can see you properly now. In that pub on the way here I couldn't see you properly because the sun was in my eyes.'

'I'm just relieved I don't have to type everything.' Hillary mimed hitting a keyboard. 'How is your *Guinness*?' she typed on the bar table.

'Bloody lovely!' Nicky typed back. And they both laughed.

The evening wore on. Both women liked to drink and they were now on their fourth pint. They were relishing each other's company.

'We could go horse riding one day if you like,' suggested Hillary. 'Have you ever been on a horse?'

'Once or twice on my sister's horses. I'm not really a good horsewoman.'

'I joined the school horse riding club when I was twelve,' said Hillary. 'We were all really scared of the woman who ran it who was a sergeant major type. This one day, it must have been only my second time there, she told me to climb up into the cab of a horsebox that was parked in the yard and fetch her a head-collar. Well, I didn't know what one was. I later found out it was a simple version of a bridle with fewer straps. I was too frightened to say I didn't know what it was. I figured it must be a kind of cloth thing that went over a horse's head. I'd seen horses with coloured things on their heads on Ivanhoe so I figured I was looking for a sort of shaped hood with holes for eyes. Well I clambered around in this cab for ages and I couldn't see any such thing, then I spotted a leather hood with holes in it. Trouble was it was all tangled up in the gear stick. It took me ages to wrestle it free, and all the time I was disentangling it I was worried she'd be angry because I was taking so long. Well eventually I got it free. And ran up to her holding it up triumphantly.

She looked at me, speechless for a moment and then she roared "You stupid girl what have you bought me this for?" It turned out I'd brought her the leather cover that goes over the gear stick.'

The two of them laughed hysterically for several minutes.

'No wonder it took you so long to disentangle it!' gasped Nicky.

'Yes!' laughed Hillary. 'I had a hell of a job yanking it off. I don't think she fully understood why I had started to dismantle the lorry, and she treated me like a simpleton after that.'

Their loud laughter drew stares from the other drinkers.

'Have you noticed how most of the couples in here are staring at us?' asked Nicky.

'Ah,' grinned Hillary, 'all the women are jealous.'

The two women broke into fresh paroxysms of laughter when Hillary went to the bar to buy the next round. The bar was quiet enough for everyone to hear the barman say 'That will be three pounds sixty please, sir.'

It was that kind of evening. Everything conspired to make them laugh uproariously.

'Do you think we should head up to the room? It's half one,' Hillary asked.

'Yeah, but lets be naughty and take a pint each up to the room.' Nicky went to the bar and Hillary went to the lift heading for the room. She wanted to clean her teeth and freshen up. Remarkably, with her poor sense of direction Hillary found the room but could not make the electronic key work in the door. Like a fool she was still standing there fumbling when Nicky appeared carrying a tray.

'So...' laughed Nicky easing the card in easily and opening the door. 'You can't tell a head collar from a gear stick cover and you can't open hotel doors. Is there anything else I should know about you?' They went in and closed the door. The room felt wonderfully luxurious. Nicky put the beer down and Hillary delved in her rucksack till she found the portable CD player and mini speakers that she had brought. She put a CD in and 'Your love is King' by Sade started playing. Hillary had never had any doubts about how she would feel when she got Nicky alone. Walking over to where Nicky stood by the dressing table she put her arms around Nicky's waist.

'I'm so glad you are here,' she said and kissed Nicky very gently on the mouth. Nicky's skin felt beautifully soft next to her cheek. Nicky's arms went round Hillary's neck. They started moving slowly round to the music as they kissed.

*

Nicky awoke first the next morning. The previous night they had, with many giggles filled in the little card to leave on their doorknob with their breakfast order. An attack of the munchies had seen to it that they ordered practically everything on the menu. Hillary did not stir when the soft knock came and Nicky slipped on her jeans and T-shirt and opened the door to allow the maid to carry the large tray in. Nicky arranged the plates of sausage, bacon, eggs and tomatoes on the little table by the window and set out knives, forks, cups, cereal and two glasses of orange juice. Then she poured them both a cup of tea and brought Hillary's to her bedside.

'Morning darling, here's a cup of tea.'

Hillary opened her eyes and saw Nicky perched beside her on the bed, then took in the cup of tea, the luxurious room and the table set for breakfast. She took hold of Nicky's hand.

'I've woken up in heaven,' she said.

They ate a lovely breakfast sitting opposite each other on two plush chairs. As they ate Nicky studied the map of the area.

'I think we should attempt the main scenic drive today, while we've got the weather on our side,' she said.

'Okay,' said Hillary 'but I'd like to have a little walk round the town first if that's alright with you.'

Hillary took the first shower and Nicky sat back in the chair allowing the sun streaming through the window to warm her. She was going to take every bit of pleasure she could from this holiday and not worry about the future. London seemed a lifetime away already.

The two women walked around the little town. It was filled with craft shops crammed with trinkets and lots of seafood restaurants. They found a shop selling leather friendship bracelets and Nicky quite unselfconsciously tied both her own and Hillary's onto their wrists right there in the shop. Hillary knew Nicky had come out when she was nineteen so she must be a lot more used to going around as a couple with another woman than Hillary was. Last night Hillary had said "Individually we both look like lesbians, but put us together and there's no doubt about it."

'You'll get used to it,' Nicky had replied.

Now they were on the scenic drive. The small roads wound their way through the mountains with spectacular coastal views. The sea was a very deep blue with the sun twinkling on the waves. Nicky was a good and careful driver. She smoked as she drove along.

'What do Peter and Isabel think about you coming on this holiday?' asked Nicky.

'Well Peter's delighted. He's made me promise to tell him "all the gory details" when I get back. Isabel told me not to get my hopes up too high and to just enjoy it as much as possible. How about your friends?'

'They all think I'm completely mad! I had to promise to send them all e-mails so they know you're not an axe murderer. Imogen in particular thinks it's an insane thing to do, to go on holiday with someone you don't know.'

'Dermot rang this morning when you were in the shower,' said Hillary.

'God! Did he? What did he say?'

'I didn't answer it. He'd probably only just found the note I left. I put on it "Gone on holiday with Peter, back in eight days". I must be the only woman in

Ireland who has to lie to her husband that she's with a man when she's actually with a woman!'

Hillary and Nicky came back tired and happy from their drive. They enjoyed succulent steaks in the hotel bar then settled down to more drinks.

'This was the very seat I was sitting in when I came out to Peter,' said Hillary. 'I had thought the booth next door was empty so spoke in a normal voice. When I'd got to the end, four women emerged and gave us a long look as they passed us!'

Nicky laughed. 'I bet you made their night with that story!'

The days passed quickly. Hillary took Nicky down to the sea wall one day and they sat and talked. 'This was where I sat with Peter a year ago and vowed I'd find a girlfriend and bring her back here for a romantic holiday.'

'Yes, and you made it happen. How does it feel?'

'It feels wonderful.'

Later that day Hillary fulfilled another ambition and took Nicky out on a boat to see the wild but friendly Dolphin that lived in Ballybay harbour. Nicky was thrilled and took lots of pictures.

Before they knew it their last day was upon them. They drove towards Hillary's hometown and stopped about forty miles short of it, booking into a four-star hotel they had seen in the guidebook as a treat. Nicky had a morning flight so they would book an early alarm call at the hotel and Nicky would then drop Hillary off and head to Dublin airport. The hotel was a converted castle and had looked very romantic in the guidebook. However, as they walked into the foyer they knew they had made a mistake. An array of dead animals' heads, foxes and stags adorned the wall along with hunting prints. The male uniformed receptionist looked down his nose at them and asked them twice 'Was that a double room, Madam?' They were not allowed to park the car at the front of the castle because cars were aesthetically unpleasing. They had to park around the back. A porter in a bright red uniform helped carry their luggage all the way round the hotel and up to their room. After he put their bags down he stood looking at Nicky who gave him two pound coins.

'I've never done that before,' grinned Nicky.

The room was incredibly old fashioned, and not a patch on the room they had left that morning. Hillary arranged her wash things in the cramped bathroom while Nicky sat on the bed and read the leather bound information book about the hotel. There was no television in the room. Beside the bed were a very sharp pencil and some paper.

'I don't think we'll be eating here, babe,' called Nicky. 'Listen to this: "Guests are required to dress for dinner. We expect the gentlemen to look smart and the ladies to complement them."'

'I can see into the dining room from here!' shouted Hillary excitedly. 'The serving staff are in penguin suits and there are women in there with long dresses on!'

'Oh Lord! It's Silver Service then,' said Nicky.

'Shall we check out the bar?' asked Hillary coming back into the room. They went back downstairs. In their jeans and T-shirts they clashed with the other guests milling about who were dressed formally. The bar was completely empty. The same man who had checked them in at reception slipped behind the bar and took their orders. He did not smile or welcome them in any way. As he got the drinks Hillary leaned over to Nicky and whispered, 'We don't like your type around here, gringo!'

Suddenly a little man rushed in, sat at the piano behind them and started playing 'Feelings' while the barman eyed them sullenly. The two women dared not look at each other for fear of bursting into laughter. Nicky put her mouth to Hillary's ear and said 'I feel like we are in a sit-com!'

'Will you be dining with us, madam?' the man asked Nicky.

'No, we thought we'd check out the village, thank you,' she answered.

'I can save you the trouble. It's a scruffy little place.'

Nicky was speechless at this. They finished their drinks, went outside and burst out laughing.

'What a place!' said Nicky.

'It's certainly an experience,' replied Hillary as they climbed into the car and headed for the village. They found a small hotel that was more the type of place they should have booked into and asked if they could eat.

'Do we just go and sit down or will you call us?' asked Nicky.

'Well, you see, people leave...' said the little shrew-faced woman inexplicably and moved off.

They sat themselves in the dining room and ordered steak and chips. The food was really delicious.

They ordered beer and after a while it became apparent to Hillary that the blonde waitress in a black dress and white apron was flirting with her. She wondered if Nicky had noticed and if it might be annoying her.

'I'll just put your beer down here, okay?' said the waitress bending down and looking deep into Hillary's eyes.

'My God, have you seen the way that woman is looking at you?' said Nicky when she'd gone.

'Yes. Are you jealous?'

Nicky leaned across the table and briefly took Hillary's hand. 'No. I'm proud.'

Hillary sipped her iced cold *Budweiser* and thought she couldn't be happier. Here she was, sitting having a delicious meal with the woman of her dreams and the pretty waitress was flirting with her. She felt like a king.

After their meal they drifted to a small pub where they sat on bar stools facing each other and sipping pints. Hillary began telling Nicky about her friends Peter, Phil (whom she had not come out to yet), and Isabel. After she had talked for a while she began to ask Nicky about her friends but Nicky clammed up and was very uncommunicative. Hillary was just wondering what was wrong when she realised Nicky had tears in her eyes.

'Oh babe, are you thinking about going home?' Hillary asked. Nicky nodded and a small tear fell onto her hand. 'Do you want to get some beer and go back to the room?' Nicky nodded again.

Smuggling the beer up to the room set them off laughing again. Hillary was relieved to see Nicky's mood lighten. When they let themselves back into the room the light was on.

'Someone's been in here,' said Hillary straight away. 'We didn't leave the light on.'

'Oh look, someone's turned down the bed,' said Nicky. 'I hope it made old Poker-Face cringe picturing us rolling about in there.'

Hillary spotted two new objects on the dressing table that hadn't been there before.

'Look they've left us something.' She picked one up. 'Posh eye blinds!' They've left us one each, so one can sleep if the other is reading.' She tested hers out holding it up to her eyes. 'Mine's too big. Do you think we can keep them?' Nicky was rolling on the bed in silent mirth.

'Hillary,' she managed to say. 'Those are the curtain ties.'

Nicky was reading the hotel guide again. ' "If any guest especially wishes to hear a radio program, arrangements may be made at reception for a radiogram to be available." ' She read. 'My God, what century are these people in?'

' "Smoking is not encouraged in the rooms but if guests must smoke they should open the windows as smoking may set off the fire alarm." We'd better open the window.' Nicky went to the window, which only opened at the top and had thick ivy growing all around it. The window came open with a thump although Nicky tried to open it quietly as the hotel unbelievably had been in darkness when they came in. The whole place made you want to tiptoe around; it was as quiet as a grave. Immediately a shrieking emerged from outside the window and a dozen creatures came from the ivy and began battering themselves against the window. Hillary knew Nicky was frightened of bats and flying insects and rushed to shut it straight away as Nicky reeled backwards. The little birds, for that is what they were, continued to beat against the window squealing as they did so.

'Are we staying in *Fawlty Towers*?' gasped Nicky.

They settled down on the bed and soon became serious again. Hillary took Nicky in her arms and the tears came again.

'You will see me again you know,' said Hillary softly.

'I know,' said Nicky. 'I just need to have a little cry.'

*

When the telephone rang with their alarm call Hillary was already awake. Nicky lay in her arms, cuddled close. They both felt sad now, as they took showers and packed. The hotel had been unable to provide breakfast before eight o' clock.

'That's the worst hundred and thirty quid I ever spent,' said Hillary.

'Oh don't worry. I got our own back,' said Nicky with a small grin. 'Remember those three lesbian magazines I bought for you to read? Well I left them on the table in the foyer tucked in behind all those copies of *Horse and Hound*.'

Nicky pulled two cans of energy drink from her rucksack.

'We'd better have these seeing as we have had no breakfast.'

It was a sunny morning and the two women would have loved to take their time as they drove along. Instead they had to hurry. Nicky had a plane to catch.

Hillary put her cap on again and hid behind the map as they drove past Dermot's office. His car was outside so at least Hillary would have time to unpack and gather her thoughts before she had to face him.

Nicky pulled up outside Hillary's house. Once again Nicky had tears in her eyes.

'Goodbye, darling,' said Hillary, kissing Nicky softly. 'Have a safe journey home. I love you.'

With that she got out of the car and went into the house, without looking back. Nicky drove round the corner into the quiet lane, leaned back in her seat and wept.

CHAPTER 5

Timber was beside himself with delight when Hillary opened the door. Hillary put her rucksack down, clipped on his lead and took him straight out for a walk.

They headed down the long straight lane towards the lake. Dry stone walls bordered the road on either side. Sheep grazed in the fields. Luckily Timber had never bothered with sheep and passed them as though they were trees.

Hillary felt in a bit of a daze. Getting up so early was part of the reason. But also it was a shock to have gone from being with Nicky all the time back to being alone again. She thought of Dermot then deliberately pushed that thought to the back of her mind. Being with Nicky had been like being in a film. She had felt really alive for the first time in ages. She had laughed more in a week than she had done for years. Nicky had far exceeded her expectations as a person. She was so gentle, so thoughtful.

As she walked, her feet making a rhythm that was trance-like, she thought of how Nicky had held doors open for her, and regularly asked her was she okay? Was she warm enough? It had been many years since Hillary had been treated with consideration like that. It had felt so good. And to sleep next to a sweet-smelling woman whom you actually loved to be next to had been heaven. The sex too had been wonderful, but this was secondary in her recollections of her time spent with Nicky. She thought of how men treated lesbianism like it was all about hot girl on girl action. There was so much more to it than that. A love affair between two women was a thing of beauty. She knew that now first hand. She felt blessed.

They were at the lake now and Hillary let Timber off the lead to run around. As he splashed in the shallows she thought how much she would like to scoop Timber up and run after Nicky's car and for them all to go back to Ballybay together. But this was not a film. Nicky was on her way back to the airport now and in a few hours she would be back in London. As she walked back to the house Hillary typed a text message to Nicky, holding the phone in one hand and typing with her thumb, *I love you.*

Within seconds the answer came back; *I love you too.*

Hillary let herself in the back door and took her first good look around the kitchen. The sink was piled high with dishes and the draining boards on either side were also covered in cups, plates and glasses. It didn't surprise Hillary that Dermot had deemed washing up to be beneath him. The same thing had happened when she had gone away with Peter. With a small laugh she saw that amongst the pile were plastic plates, cups and cutlery. Dermot had obviously run out of clean dishes and began to use their picnic set. The washing machine was packed so full she could barely get her hands in and she had to wash the contents in two lots. In the bathroom the sink was full of empty toilet roll holders. The fire was filled to the top of the grate with ashes. 'This is not a home,' thought Hillary. 'Whatever it is it's not a home.'

She had plenty of housework to do to keep her busy. She felt sad unpacking the outfits she had worn on holiday, as she remembered where she was when she had worn each one. When she had finished all her work Hillary had a long bath with plenty of bubbles in it. Then she lit a big fire, made herself some cheese on toast and sat down to watch some television. The dog lay on the rug, happy that there was a fire to lie in front of again.

Suddenly at seven o'clock, Hillary looked out of the window to see Dermot's *Land Rover* parked in front of the five-barred gate. The shock of it made her jump. Her adrenaline started pumping. Timber sensed her fear right away and started barking. Even if he couldn't see inside the house from where he was, Dermot would know she was home because the gate was shut. Laziness made him always leave it open so he could drive straight in. Hillary thought it looked like Dermot was talking on his mobile phone but she couldn't be sure at this distance. He sat there for fifteen long minutes revving his engine, staring into the room where Hillary sat shaking. Finally he reversed, turned round and set off up the lane to the pub. Hillary was in no doubt what this message meant. He had come home to check she was back. She had said eight days in her note and today was Tuesday again. He had wanted her to sit there shaking, afraid he would come in. But he would drink himself into a state about it first. He wanted her to sweat.

All of the cosiness had seeped out of the room. Hillary lit a cigarette and started pacing. She picked up her mobile phone and typed a text to Nicky; *Can you come on the computer now.* She logged on and waited.

At last Topcat's name appeared in her little buddy list window.

'Hi.' typed Hillary. 'How was your flight home?'

'It was fine,' said Nicky. 'Jack picked me up from the airport and had Bruce in the car as a surprise.'

Bruce was Nicky's beloved old English pointer.

'Any sign of D yet?'

'He just appeared at the gate, sat there revving his engine for fifteen minutes staring into the house then drove off to the pub.'

'Oh God' typed Nicky. 'When he comes back don't say anything to make him angry.'

'I don't' think I'll need to. He looked angry enough.'

'Just be careful, babe. Make sure you have Timber in the room with you.'

'Well I'm planning to be in bed when he gets home but he'll probably wake me up,' typed Hillary.

'I just wish I was there to protect you.'

*

Hillary lay awake in bed. The room smelled of beer and the duvet was slightly damp because the central heating did not work properly. She heard the *Land Rover* stop outside the gate. Then there was a pause while Dermot got out to open the gate and then the sound of him accelerating up to the back door. She could hear the loud music he always had playing in his car and the sound of Timber barking. The bedside clock said it was two-fifteen. She didn't have to wait long. The bedroom door flew open and Dermot entered the room switching on the light. Hillary tried to look as if she were just waking up.

'No you don't, you devious little bitch,' he slurred suddenly reaching under the duvet and pulling at her ankle. 'Don't think you can hide in here and pretend you're asleep. You've got some talking to do.'

He pulled her by the ankle right out of the bed. Hillary just managed to reach out with her hands and stop her chin from hitting the floor. Without a word she got up off the floor and walked passed him into the living room.

'So just exactly what's going on here? That's twice now you've run off with Mister Bloody Peter Brennan without a word. Do you think I'm a fool?'

'I went on a summer holiday like I did last year. I know you don't want to go so there's no point in asking you, is there?' said Hillary shivering in her pyjamas with her back to the fire.

'If you'd asked me I would have let you go. There was no need to go off like a sneaky thief without a word. Now just what is going on here? Are you planning on leaving me for him or what?'

'You know I've been friends with Peter since I was eighteen. There is nothing going on. He has a nice girlfriend called Sarah. He came over to visit his brother and we spent some time in Ballybay. We went out to see the dolphin a few times, walked round the junk shops. All the things you hate doing. It was the only way I was going to get a holiday this year. It's normal. Everyone goes on holiday.'

'It's not normal to go with another man. Well Missy, there are going to be some big changes around here. I work eighteen hours a day to keep you in luxury so you can talk to your boyfriend on the internet all night running up huge phone bills. Get to bed. I don't want to even look at your lying ugly little face anymore. Just fuck off out of my sight. Run to Peter. I don't give a fuck.'

Hillary went back to bed. She knew Dermot would be hours yet. He always came home ravenous from the pub and would sit in front of the television eating huge bowls of ice cream and packets of crisps and chocolate, and he would always fall asleep in the chair. He would wake up when he got cold at around five in the morning and stagger to bed. She snuggled down under the duvet trying to find some warmth there. She had got off very lightly. Very lightly indeed.

*

Dermot had been huffy for the rest of the week but it was nothing compared to what she had been expecting. It was quite possible he had missed having his 'maid' around and was just happy that she was back and apparently staying. When she had returned from her holiday with Peter he hadn't spoken to her for a week.

On Friday evening Hillary settled down at the computer looking for Nicky. She felt sure now that they had become so much closer on the holiday that Nicky would be here. But there was no sign of her.

Hillary talked to her friend Jemm who was in Perth, Australia. She told her all about the holiday and what a wonderful time she had had.

'I'm so pleased for you, Dove. What plans have you made for the future? Are you moving in together soon?'

Hillary read the sentence and it made her feel uncomfortable. The truth was that Nicky had not once mentioned the future and Hillary had felt somehow afraid to bring it up. She knew what was behind this fear. She was afraid that any talk of the future would frighten her away. Hillary looked for Nicky many times that weekend but to no avail. She didn't want to text her and appear demanding. Finally on Sunday evening she received an e-mail.

Hi Gorgeous,
I'm over at Dan's across the road borrowing his computer. My phone has been cut off because I didn't pay the bill. Missing you like crazy. Sorry I can't afford to ring on the mobile. I'm hoping to get it re-connected as soon as possible. Hope your weekend went well.
Lotsa Love, Nicky x x x

*

On August the seventeenth it was Nicky's birthday. By a strange quirk of fate it was also Dermot's birthday. Dermot didn't let Hillary out of his sight when they were shopping, but it was easy to escape from him to choose Nicky's present on the pretext of choosing something for Dermot. She bought Dermot a fishing book, as he was a very keen fisherman. For Nicky's present, she went into a little antique shop that had just opened in her village. She found a beautiful little statuette of a naked woman reclining with one hand under her head. The woman was petite and had short hair with a fringe like Hillary's. Hillary knew the bronze statuette would remind Nicky of her. The German lady working in the shop had told her it was an original from the nineteen twenties. She also bought Nicky a *Zippo* lighter with a Celtic design on it.

The parcel arrived right on time on the actual day of Nicky's birthday but they could not spend it together. Nicky was spending the day going out for a posh meal with her friends and in the evening, drinking with them in her local pub. Hillary felt obliged to go out with Dermot on his birthday. It was the first time she had been out anywhere since the holiday in July and she felt nervous and tense all night. She knew it was irrational but she half expected someone to tap her on the shoulder and say 'Hi Hillary, I hear you are having a lesbian affair'. She now had a very butch haircut, but she tried to femme herself up for the evening by wearing a rather girlie blouse.

Dermot had drunk even more than usual and when he came home he immediately fell asleep in his chair. The alcohol made Hillary feel brave. Certain that Dermot would not wake up she opened a can of beer from the fridge and carried it into the room they called 'the office' where the computer was.

She placed two pillows over the modem as it screeched its way onto the internet. When she logged onto her messenger she was thrilled to see Topcat's name on her buddy list. It was two thirty am.

'Hi,' she typed. 'Happy birthday. How was your night?' There was a very long pause. Finally a phrase popped up.

'I'm drunk'.

'Lol, I bet you are. Did you have a good time, birthday girl?' Another long pause.

'My legs were drunk in the pub.'

'Did you get any nice presents?' Hillary typed.

'I've got something to tell you,' Nicky typed at length.

'What?'

'It's just...It's just I'm drunk'

'Lol, I know you are. You are allowed to be drunk it's your birthday! You get yourself to bed now. Don't be up typing in the cold. I'll see you tomorrow.'

'OK.'

'Goodnight, sweet girl. I love you. Happy birthday.'

'Night.'

*

The rest of the summer passed uneventfully. Hillary was happier now that she had met Nicky, even though Nicky spent less time online than she used to. Hillary spent many long hours sawing logs for the fire from the branches that littered the garden. It was now autumn and both women were desperate to meet again. It was Nicky who came up with an idea one night when they were relaxing together on the phone.

'Do you remember those self-catering cottages in Ballybay by the seafront?' asked Nicky. 'Well wouldn't it be great to have a winter holiday in one of those?'

'Oh yes!' said Hillary straight away. 'That would be fab! It would be like playing house being there with you.'

'Well I've looked into it. It's really cheap at this time of year. Just under two hundred quid for a week.

How do you fancy going there on the thirtieth of November?'

'Oh babe I'd love it.'

'The cottages have got open fires. Imagine sitting by a roaring fire together.'

'It would be great,' enthused Hillary. 'I always fancied a winter holiday playing *Ludo* or *Scrabble* while the wind and rain lashed outside.'

'I love paying board games,' said Nicky.

'How about jigsaws? Do you like doing jigsaws?'

'Yes I do. Most of all I'd love to cook you some proper meals. I know all you eat is beans on toast and cheese on toast. I have a fantasy of cooking you a Sunday roast with Yorkshire pudding, roast potatoes and gravy.'

'What about television? Do the cottages come with one?'

'Yes they do,' replied Nicky.

'Hey! I could bring that old video recorder we have in the attic. It's a bit temperamental but it works.'

'Well that would be perfect. I've got a whole selection of lesbian videos I'm sure you'd love.'

'Oh lets do it! Let's just do it and sod the consequences! It would be worth any kind of hassle with Dermot to have a week like that.'

CHAPTER 6

The thirtieth of November was only seven days away. Hillary spent a happy and frenzied week collecting all the things she thought they would need in the cottage. It was like preparing for a life together but in miniature. Seven wrapped fire lighters. Two bags of small logs which she had cut and dried on the range. Five turf briquettes in another bag to get the first fire going. A little bottle of cooking oil she had dispensed from the big bottle. A little bottle of fabric softener. Seven washing powder tablets. Sachets of ketchup, salt and vinegar which she had saved from trips to fast food outlets. Toilet rolls, tissues and bin-bags. Teabags and small individual cartons of orange juice. A packet of digestives and a six pack of *Kit-Kats*. She sang as she assembled these things and laughed to herself when she thought what Dermot would have made of this collection if he had found it.

Nicky flew over and hired a car as she had done last time. Hillary assembled all her bags out in the front garden behind the tree by the road, including their old video recorder, which was in a large bin-bag to protect it from the dew. Once again she hoped for a quick get-away. She didn't want to bump into any of her neighbours while hauling this stash into Nicky's hire car.

She had a bad moment when the doorbell rang just as she was heaving her last bag down the ladder from the attic. It was Richard, Dermot's business partner who had called to collect a roll of fax paper. He was very chatty but if he noticed Hillary's edgy manner he didn't say anything. Hillary knew that if there was a car outside when Nicky arrived, Nicky would drive round the block until it had gone.

Now she was hovering outside in her front garden when the text came: *D's car there, on my way.*

Within minutes a white *Ford Fiesta* hove into view. Nicky knew Hillary would have more luggage this time and she hopped out and helped throw the bags into the boot. Hillary jumped into the back and they were away.

It had been four months since they had seen each other but it felt like four days. The two women settled into an easy conversation.

'Have you brought the videos?'

'Yes. Have you brought the recorder?'

'I've brought cooking oil.'

'I've brought a flask.'

The journey to Ballybay didn't seem like hard work at all, so happy were the women in each other's company. They only stopped once for a cup of tea. Nicky didn't want to be driving for too much of the journey in the dark. As they descended the long hill into the little town Hillary said, 'Remember when you stopped on this hill on the way in last time because of that bee and I thought you'd decided you couldn't go through with it?'

Nicky laughed. 'Yes, I do you daft bat!'

Nicky collected the key from a nearby lodge as she had been instructed. The little holiday cottages, which were newly built, were arranged in a horseshoe shape facing the sea. They were painted white and each had a different coloured front door. Only one cottage had a car in the drive. Not many people wanted a holiday by the sea in the first week of December. Nicky's key fob said number four. The outside light had been left on to welcome them. They opened the door and went inside. The cottage was beautifully furnished with a brand new fitted kitchen and large dining table. Hillary and Nicky began unpacking the car right away, eagerly taking in all the little goodies each other had brought. When all the bags were emptied out Hillary went into the lounge and lit a roaring fire whilst Nicky connected up the video recorder. Then Nicky stood up and embraced Hillary as tightly as she could.

'It's so good to feel you again,' she whispered into Hillary's cheek. They made love in front of the fire, losing themselves in each other.

Hillary ran a hot bath and they took it in turns to soap each other, washing away all traces of the long journey. Then they sat on the sofa cuddled up together drinking cold beer and watched a film that Nicky had brought.

After the film Hillary threw some more logs onto the fire and snuggled up next to Nicky again.

'I couldn't be happier at this moment,' she said stroking Nicky's arm. 'You were so clever to think of this cottage. It's just perfect.'

'It's amazing to think I was in London this morning,' said Nicky. 'And now here I am in Ballybay with my beautiful girl.'

'It's like Christmas has come early,' murmured Hillary. 'What would you like to do tomorrow?'

'I'd quite like to go out on the boat to see the dolphin again, but this time all wrapped up in winter woollies.'

*

Hillary awoke first the next morning. Nicky's hair was spread out across the pillow and she breathed silently and gently as she slept. Nicky did not stir as Hillary quietly got out of bed and carried her clothes downstairs to dress in the living room. She let herself out noiselessly and walked to the little paper shop. She bought a daily newspaper, some bacon, sausage, eggs, milk, bread, butter and orange juice, and walked back taking deep breaths of the fresh sea air. Hillary wasn't much of a cook but she managed to rustle up a decent breakfast and carried it up to Nicky. She kissed her awake.

'Happy breakfast time sleeping beauty,' she said. Then she went back downstairs, carried up her own breakfast and got back into bed beside Nicky. They read the paper spread out between them on top of the duvet.

'I wonder what Timber and Bruce are doing?' said Hillary.

'Probably wishing someone would take them for a walk.'

They finished their breakfast and showered and dressed. Hillary washed the breakfast things then boiled the kettle and laid out two clean cups with teabags and spoons in.

'Oh, are we having more tea before we go out?' asked Nicky.

'No, that's just ready for us when we get back.'

Nicky slipped her arms around Hillary's waist from behind. 'It's lovely being here with you, watching you carry out your little domestic routines, you are so sweet pottering about in the kitchen.'

Hillary turned and embraced Nicky. Planting small kisses on her neck she said 'Make an honest woman of me and you'll get to see me doing this everyday.' Nicky looked deep into her eyes and kissed her long and hard.

They donned waterproof jackets and went out into the now steadily falling rain. There was an aquatic centre just up the road from the cottages and they had decided to give it a visit. Brightly coloured fish of all shapes and sizes were housed in various aquariums. Solemnly they read out the details to each other from the little cards. The centrepiece of the attraction was a little tunnel you walked through with large fish swimming all around and above you. Hillary and Nicky had never seen a shark up close before. The shark grinned and stared at them with his beady eyes.

Next, they walked around the trinket shops. Hillary gasped with delight when she found a paperweight that was a little glass dome with a snowstorm inside when you shook it. A Perspex insert meant that you could insert your own photograph to be in the middle of the snow. Hillary bought it and tucked it into her pocket.

They went back to the cottage to fetch the car and took off for the strand about four miles away where a famous film scene had been filmed. When they got out of the car the wind was up and blew cascades of rain into their faces.

'I'm determined to dip my toe into the Atlantic,' shouted Nicky above the roar of the wind, 'and you are coming with me!' It was a well-known joke between them that Hillary felt the cold easily, while Nicky would stride ahead like a seasoned adventurer into any storm. They battled their way down the beach. Hillary clung to Nicky's arm. Three quarters of the way down to the waters' edge they had to give up and turn back. They ran up the beach laughing to a small beach café and flung themselves in, shaking the water off them like dogs. They ordered a portion of chips each with lashings of salt and vinegar and sat in the window eating them looking out at the weather. No one else was in the café (probably because nobody else was crazy enough to visit the beach on such a day) and they played footsie with each other under the table. Hillary had noticed that Nicky was more romantic and relaxed than she had been on the previous holiday. She seemed more 'in love' and spent a lot of time gazing into Hillary's eyes.

They drove back to the house and changed out of their wet clothes. Their mood was playful. As they rubbed themselves with towels Nicky said, 'It was all because of wimpy you that we had to turn back. If I'd had a decent girlfriend she would have come all the way down to the sea with me. Now I have to go back home and I can't tell my friends I've had my toe in the Atlantic!'

Hillary turned to Nicky. 'Wimpy is it I am now? I'll show you who's wimpy!' She jumped on Nicky's back and wrestled her to the floor. She was a lot smaller than Nicky but was strong for her size. Giggling, she pinned Nicky's wrists to the floor above her head, placed her knees on Nicky's biceps and began tickling her. Nicky squirmed shouting 'No! No!'

'Say, "I defer to your greater and most wonderful power!" Say it! Say it!'

Suddenly Hillary stopped tickling and moved her face closer to Nicky's. She traced her finger along the side of Nicky's nose, up and across her forehead. There was a prominent blue line like a varicose vein standing out angrily on Nicky's face.

'What's that?' she asked incredulously. Nicky flushed and turned her head to one side.

'It's an old war wound,' she said flatly. Hillary drew her knees back so she was now just sitting astride Nicky's hips.

'What do you mean? It looks like your sinus is all inflamed.'

Nicky's face was red and she started to get up turning her face away. 'I used to do coke. It kind of left that part of my face tender and swollen.'

'My God. That's terrible,' said Hillary. 'I can't understand why I never noticed it before. When did you stop?'

'Haven't done it for over a year now,' said Nicky standing up and towelling her hair again. Her voice was flat and impersonal. 'Is it very obvious?'

'Well it kind of looks like your sinus is swollen and inflamed. There's a bulge just by your eye.' Hillary was trying hard to assimilate this new information.

'Yeah, I think it affected the sight in my right eye a bit.'

'Why didn't you tell me before?'

'I know you hate drugs. I'm not proud of it.'

69

'Did you take anything else?' Hillary was sitting stock still on the floor now.

'Just a bit of hash.'

'But you are fully stopped now right?'

There was a long silence. Nicky put her hand on Hillary's shoulder.

'It's in my past Hillary. Okay?'

*

Hillary was subdued for the rest of the evening although she tried hard to hide it from Nicky. She couldn't stop thinking about the fact that this woman she was in love with had hard drugs in her past. It was like a slap in the face. Like someone had said to her 'You see? You just don't know what you're getting into when you run off with someone off the internet.' Hillary had led a sheltered life and had never even met anyone who smoked hash, never mind anything stronger. 'My God, it's cocaine. That's serious stuff,' she thought to herself. And yet she loved Nicky with all her heart. It was wrong of her to hold this against her. She tried to imagine Nicky snorting cocaine and found it impossible. They were on the sofa now watching another video. Nicky was quiet, possibly sensing Hillary's mood. 'Grow up,' she told herself. 'People have pasts. It doesn't change who she is now.'

She reached over to Nicky and drew her into her arms. 'Come here to me little thing,' she said smiling. 'I'm lonely.'

*

70

The next day Nicky and Hillary took the boat trip out to see the dolphin. They joined a dozen others crowded onto the little fishing boat as it chugged its way out into the natural harbour. Hillary leaned against the rail and Nicky stood close behind her. They had to resist the urge to hold hands. All heads scanned the surface of the sea as the boat bobbed up and down until a voice cried 'There he is!' and everyone rushed to the same rail. The handsome creature leaped in and out of the water over and over again as the boat turned small circles on the sea. Hillary snuggled deeper inside her jacket as the wind blew spray into her face. She was frozen but determined to watch the dolphin for as long as she could, rather than shelter in the small cabin. Nicky found the cold sea spray exhilarating.

Back on dry land they visited shops selling hand knitted woollen jumpers. Nicky asked Hillary to help her to choose one with a cable pattern as a thank you to Jack for taking care of Bruce.

They walked back to the little cottage and Hillary built another big fire.

'I'm going to cook you my Special Tea tonight.' She told Nicky. There was much laughter in the kitchen as Hillary mixed a tin of meatballs with a tin of beans and seriously added salt, pepper and ketchup as if she were a master chef. The meal was hot and welcome after they day out in the cold. They sat companionably at the table. Nicky had her favourite *Elton John* playing on the CD player and speakers.

'Just think; if you lived with me you could eat like this everyday,' joked Hillary.

'I could live here quite happily and not go home,' said Nicky. But the conversation never progressed any further than that and Hillary didn't say what she wanted to say; which was 'Let's talk about that. About when we are going to be together'.

Hillary made a dessert that was impossibly sweet and Nicky made a good effort to eat it before they gave up, laughing. They washed up and dried together side by side. Hillary loved the closeness she felt doing simple domestic chores together. One of the things she enjoyed most on that holiday was washing and ironing Nicky's clothes, lovingly placing them back in the drawers for her.

Hillary took the stale loaf out of the bread bin. She handed the bread to Nicky while she began cleaning the bread bin and said, 'Take this out into the garden and give it to the birds.'

Nicky hovered for a second and went outside with the bread. Hillary could see her through the window standing in the garden looking hesitant. A few seconds later she was back.

'Do you want me to just dump it down in one pile or shall I scatter it about?'

Hillary put her arms round Nicky, smiling.

'Oh babe, you are just so sweet the way you want to please me all the time.'

*

It was now their last day and as with the summer holiday they had decided to break up the return journey by spending their last night in a hotel not too far from Hillary's home. This time they had selected a cheaper one. It turned out to be a little too cheap and had an eastern European feel about it.

They sat in the drab bar eating cheese sandwiches. A Christmas CD was playing and it had got stuck. Nicky mentioned it to various uninterested staff members without result, so they were obliged to escape to their room. Nicky held Hillary tight as they lay on the bed watching television, a cup of tea at each side of the bed.

CHAPTER 7

When Hillary got home the house was in the same state it had been last time. She hugged Timber for a long time and after his walk she lit the range and set about cleaning up. Dermot arrived at about seven o'clock but this time he did not refer to the fact Hillary had been away. He simply made a sandwich and went out to the pub. Hillary was back to her life that was not a life.

As Christmas approached Hillary noticed a change in Nicky. She behaved in a more loving and attentive way. She stayed in on Friday nights and spent them on the telephone with Hillary. On the last Friday night before Christmas Hillary finally heard the words she had been waiting to hear. Hillary had been saying how much she dreaded spending Christmas day with Dermot, for on that day in Ireland the pubs were closed.

Unexpectedly Nicky said, 'The next Christmas dinner you'll be having after this will be with me.'

She hadn't said how and she hadn't said when but she had said it. They were going to be together and it would be within the next twelve months.

That Christmas the weather was severe. There were heavy snowfalls and the temperature dropped to a record minus eight degrees Celsius. Nicky and Hillary said sad goodbyes as Nicky was to spend the Christmas holidays with Imogen again. Hillary felt bereft with Nicky gone.

As she and Dermot ate Christmas dinner watching a film on television, Hillary felt a new emotion for the first time. Guilt. She and Dermot had exchanged small gifts and both were making an effort to get into the spirit of Christmas. This was the last Christmas dinner she would ever have with Dermot but he didn't know that and was enjoying himself, oblivious. He wasn't a bad man all the time. She wished she could find someway of doing this without hurting him.

After dinner Hillary went down to the log store at the bottom of the garden to fetch some logs. Suddenly she heard the distinct high-pitched cry of an animal in distress. Standing on top of the high garden wall was a tiny ginger kitten. He was too small to be out on his own. He must have wandered away from his mother at one of the neighbouring farms and wandered through the wood till he reached Hillary's garden. This was the last thing Hillary needed. Another pet to worry about when her own future was so up in the air. But it was bitterly cold and she knew the little creature would not survive on his own. What was more, it was Christmas day. Hillary picked up the kitten, which started purring straight away and carried him to the shed. Timber hated cats so she made the kitten a warm bed in a cardboard box filled with shredded paper. He would have to live in here until he was older and stronger. She went into the kitchen and heated him up some milk, which he drank gratefully. She called the kitten Alfie.

It was a full two weeks before Hillary saw Nicky again on the computer. Nicky said she had had a good break down at her sister's. Hillary was just ecstatic to have Nicky available again. But her joy was short lived.

Nicky seemed to have changed over Christmas. Once again she seemed to be giving Hillary what Hillary thought of as 'the casual treatment'. She started going out all weekend again, staying off line until Monday evenings. When Hillary complained she said she thought it was unhealthy for them to spend so much time online, and encouraged Hillary to go out more. This had a hollow familiar ring to Hillary's ears. 'Why now?' she thought. 'Just when we seemed so close.'

In January Nicky was offline for a whole week. When she came back she said her telephone had been cut off again. Hillary was beginning to wonder if Nicky had serious financial problems that she wasn't facing up to. But somehow she felt it was rude of her to pry into Nicky's financial affairs.

It was now just coming up to Easter. Hillary had had a very bad dose of the flu in February and had lost weight. She looked haggard. Nicky had not once mentioned their future together since the Friday before Christmas and she had been so unreliable that Hillary no longer believed it would happen. They had been having a long distance relationship for a year and ten months. Susan, the student from Bristol and her girlfriend had asked Nicky if they could come and stay with her over Easter but Nicky had said no, she was driving to her sister's that weekend. Nicky had also just bought a new *Jeep*. Hillary thought this was a strange thing to do, coming from a woman who could barely afford to pay her phone bill. Somehow this act made Hillary feel alienated in a way she could not explain even to herself.

The weekend before Easter was important to Hillary, as she now knew Nicky would be away the following weekend. Dermot had a few fishing trips lined up with his friends so he wouldn't be around. Hillary planned to get Nicky to phone her. She was going to bite the bullet and ask Nicky just what her plans were. Even if it meant frightening Nicky away she believed she deserved to know where she stood. Nicky had agreed to stay in on Friday night. They were to meet online at seven. Hillary got a few cans of beer in for Dutch courage.

Dermot called her at six thirty to let her know he and his friends were safely off the lake and on their way to the pub. Hillary watched his *Land Rover* go by the house then she fully relaxed. Snuggling up in front of the fire with one of her beers she texted Nicky: *D gone to pub. Coast is clear to ring.*

She laid the phone on the couch next to her and took deep breaths trying to relax herself for the conversation ahead. When fifteen minutes had passed she started pacing. Another fifteen minutes went by and she decided she wasn't going to waste the whole night waiting. She would just have to call Nicky herself and once again face the risk of having Nicky's number on her phone bill. Dermot had not noticed it the last time she had done so.

She rang the number. It was engaged. Half an hour passed and she dialled again. Still engaged. She wondered if Nicky was online. She went to the computer. No Topcat. Then she took the bold step of dialling Nicky's mobile number, even though she knew this would show up in a special section of the bill entitled 'calls to foreign mobiles'. She got through to a recorded message.

'Hi it's me,' she said, her voice flat and disappointed. 'Trying to get through to you. Ring me when you get a chance.'

She had now tried every avenue. She tried to watch television to pass the rest of the night but couldn't concentrate. Finally at eleven o'clock she logged onto the computer and started talking to Jemm, who liked to chat early in the morning.

'Hi Jemm, how are you?'

'Hi Dove. I'm fine. What are you up to?

'Well Topcat was meant to ring me this evening but she hasn't and her phone is engaged. I've been trying to get hold of her all night as she's going away for Easter next weekend.'

'This isn't the first time this has happened is it?'

'No. I just don't know what's up with her.'

'You have to face it Dove, it's looking a lot like she is seeing someone else.'

'I know it looks that way but I can't believe she could be. She seems so in love with me at other times. It's just that she blows hot and cold and is often unreliable.'

'Well like I've said before you are just going to have to ask her straight out.'

'I was going to do that this evening. Well, not ask her if she was seeing anyone else but ask her what her plans are for us. I kind of got myself all geared up for it tonight and now I can't get hold of her.'

'Well,' typed Jemm, 'for your own peace of mind you must ask her as soon as you get hold of her. But do it on the phone this time. Not by e-mail.'

Hillary went to bed with a very heavy heart.

On Saturday and Sunday Hillary tried to keep herself busy. She took all the plants out of the conservatory and gave then a spring tidy up. In the evenings she did look briefly for Nicky on the computer but amused herself talking to other people about other things.

On Monday afternoon the excuse from Nicky arrived in her inbox as expected. She had to go to her sisters unexpectedly. Hillary barely read it.

For the rest of the week Hillary was evasive herself. She didn't go on the computer every night and when she did the conversations with Nicky were stilted and drawn out. Nicky asked for a special 'computer date' with Hillary on the Thursday before Easter, as she would be away for the next few days. Nicky said she would get a bottle of wine in. But Hillary made an excuse. She wasn't yet ready for the confrontation that was surely to come.

The Friday after Easter Hillary was ready. Once again she texted Nicky to call her and once again she was disappointed. This time she received a text from Nicky saying she was having phone trouble and would get on line as soon as it was sorted out. She was sorry, she said, she couldn't afford to ring on her mobile phone. The whole weekend was a repeat of the one before Easter. Including the fact that she rang Nicky's number only to find it engaged. In the conversation with Jemm on the Friday night she finally faced up to the fear that was growing inside her.

'She says she's got phone trouble,' she typed to Jemm. 'But God help me, I just don't believe her.'

'I don't think I would believe her either, Dove,' typed Jemm.

'I'm ready to face her with it. But what if I'm wrong Jemm?'

'I don't think you are wrong, Dove.'

This time the Monday e-mail was really long and involved. Nicky said the lady next door had switched her phoneline to broadband and it had affected Nicky's line because it ran through her house, it being a semi-detached. 'But this is good in the long run' Nicky had typed. 'Because it means I have broadband too, so I'll have a better internet connection'. For some reason reading the word 'broadband' was the catalyst she needed. Somehow she knew for a fact that Nicky was lying.

She didn't answer the e-mail or go online for a few days. Finally on Thursday she was ready to face it. She went on line. Topcat was waiting there. Nicky had suddenly become attentive now that Hillary had shown she could blow cold too.

'Hi darling,' typed Nicky 'I've been worried about you.'

Hillary took a huge breath. 'I don't believe you,' she typed. 'I don't believe that your phone line was down and I don't believe that you were at your sister's the weekend before Easter.'

There was a long pause. 'Well I'm sorry you don't believe me but it happens to be true.'

'I don't believe you were at your sister's for Easter weekend either,' typed Hillary. 'Your phone was engaged when I tried to call you when you were supposed to be away at Imogen's. It was engaged for hours.'

'That's Jack, he's always using the phone.'

'It was engaged when you were meant to be having broadband put in too.'

'That was the workmen trying the phoneline. You've got to believe me Hillary.'

'I haven't got to believe you and I don't. You have been giving me excuse after excuse and they are getting more and more outlandish. You are never available at weekends or public holidays. I can think of no other reason than that you are seeing someone else. So I guess it's time for me to stop being an idiot and to bow out.'

'Hillary you are wrong. I swear it,' typed Nicky.

'And what am I to make of the fact that you never speak of our future together despite us having a relationship for two years?'

'I don't have the means right now, please listen to me,' Nicky typed.

'It's nothing to do with means. The only reason I am not in your bed right now is that you've never asked me.'

'You'd hate London. You always said you don't like busy places.'

'Nicky. The game is up. I'm not playing anymore. Goodbye.' And with that Hillary logged off, rushed to her bed and sobbed as though her heart would break.

*

It was Saturday morning. Hillary sat up in bed as the awfulness of recent events rushed into her mind. Timber crawled up the bed on his belly and began to lick her face. She had managed to let the whole of Friday go by without checking her e-mail. But now it was time to look. Already she regretted all the things she had said to Nicky. She didn't really believe that Nicky was seeing someone. It was just too impossible. Hillary thought the truth was much simpler than that. Nicky just liked her independence and Hillary had been tying her down. She wondered if Nicky would ever forgive the things she had said. Still in her boxers and T-shirt she padded to the computer. Dermot had got up early and gone to fetch two of his friends to go fishing with. With trembling hands she logged on and selected her mailbox. 'Inbox 1' it said. She had expected that. But what came next was a complete shock.

Dear Hillary,

I owe you a massive apology for all the things I have done to you over the past two years. I have watched you struggle with trying to work everything out and it's been hard to watch. All I've ever given to you is lies. My whole life is a lie and I got myself in so deep I just couldn't get out of it. You are such a good and loving person and I have paid you back with deceit. I took advantage of your trusting nature. I've been an absolute bastard and I hate myself for what I've done to you. I hope you will believe me when I tell you I did it all because I loved you and feared losing you. I have seen the toll my lies have taken on you recently and I am so ashamed. But from now on all you will get from me is the truth. Text me at noon tomorrow and I will call you and tell you everything... the whole truth. I owe you that much at least to tell you in person, or as near to that as is

possible. Until then I hope you sleep well tonight knowing nothing has been your fault.
Till tomorrow, with all my love,
Nicky x x x

So. It was really true then. Nicky had been lying to her. She still found it hard to really take in; even now it was in front of her in black and white. Whatever it was it sounded serious. She looked at the clock. It was ten thirty. She grabbed her mobile and texted Jemm. *Please ring me now. Urgent.* The phone rang within a minute.

'Hi Jemm. I've just got an e-mail from her. It says she's been lying to me all along. She says she's going to call me at noon and tell me everything. I'm so scared.'

'Oh you poor thing. Well whatever it is it can't be worse than carrying on not knowing.'

'I'm certain she's in some kind of big financial trouble.'

'It's more than likely to be that she's seeing another woman. Whatever it is it's going to be bad. You've got to prepare yourself for that.'

'Oh shit, here's Dermot back with his mates. I've got to go. Bye Jemm.'

Dermot drove into the drive with his two friends on board. Hillary was in a cold sweat. She would have to go out and say hello.

It was worse than she expected. Dermot dropped off his mates then went into the village to buy food for their fishing trip. Hillary had to make small talk while the two men assembled all the fishing equipment.

'You look tired,' said one of them.

'I didn't sleep well,' said Hillary.

It was a beautiful sunny morning at the beginning of May. Sunny enough, luckily for Hillary to be able to put on her sunglasses in an attempt to hide her feelings. The two men loaded up the boat while Hillary stood in the garden, her autopilot somehow managing to keep the conversation going.

At long last Dermot returned and Hillary was able to melt into the background. They finally left at a quarter to twelve. Hillary shut the gate and went indoors. Automatically she made herself a strong cup of tea. She took out her mobile and texted, *I'm ready.*

The phone rang a few minutes later.

'Hello.'

'Hi.' Nicky sounded as if she had been crying, or indeed as if she was crying. Suddenly Dermot's *Land Rover* swept up to the front gate and he jumped out.

'Damn here's Dermot back,' Hillary said and switched the phone off and stuffed it under a cushion.

'Forgot one of the reels,' he said breathlessly as he rushed passed her.

In a few seconds he rushed passed again and went out to the car and drove away.

Coast clear, she texted to Nicky. Another few minutes passed and the phone rang again.

'So what is it?' Hillary asked. 'I'm ready to hear it whatever it is.'

There was a long pause. Then Nicky said in a tiny voice, 'I've got a coke habit, Hillary.'

Hillary thought she said 'toke habit' and said 'You've got a what?'

'I've got a coke habit.' This time Hillary heard. She tried to collect a few brain cells together for a response.

'Well, we can get you help for that. It's not the end of the world,' she finally managed. 'How bad is it?'

'It's quite bad.' Hillary knew she ought to be horrified but all she could feel was relief.

'Oh thank God, Nicky I thought you were going to say you had another woman,' she blurted out. There was a pause. A very long pause.

In a barely audible voice Nicky said 'It's not a woman.'

Wham! The sentence hit Hillary like a hammer. Its implication trickled through into Hillary's sensibilities like treacle being dripped from a wooden spoon.

'What did you say?' said Hillary.

'It's not a woman.'

'A man?' Once again the seconds ticked by.

'Yes.'

'Does he live with you?'

'Yes.' Hillary suddenly thought of them choosing the jumper in Ballybay.

'Is it Jack?'

'Yes.' Nicky was crying now. Like an idiot returning to her senses Hillary suddenly realised that Jack was not a lodger.

'How long have you been with him?'

'Twenty years.'

'Oh God.' Hillary sat down on the arm of the couch. 'Are you married?'

'No.'

'Do you sleep with him?'

'Yes.' Hillary felt all her energy being drained out of her body down her thighs and out through the bottom of her feet.

'So you are not really my girl after all,' she said woodenly.

'Oh God. I'm so sorry Hillary,' Nicky sobbed noisily.

Hillary felt strangely calm now.

'So I suppose he has a coke habit too?' she said flatly.

'Yes.' Nicky said through her sobs.

'And you can't leave him because he buys the drugs.' A worse thought hit her. 'Do you love him?'

'Yes.' Hillary leaned against the back of the couch.

'So all those weekends you are unavailable you're having coke parties with him?'

'Sometimes it's just us, but we often go to friends and do it.'

'All your friends are coke addicts as well then?'

'All except Carol and Linda.'

'What does he look like?

Nicky broke into fresh sobs. 'Oh Hillary, you don't really want to hear this.'

'I've just found out someone else is sleeping with my girlfriend,' said Hillary coldly. 'I'm at least entitled to know what he looks like.'

'He's tall. About six-one, with black hair and glasses. Hillary, I kept meaning to tell you. But the longer it went on the harder it got.'

'So you just decided it would be okay to play with my life for two years. String me along and make me believe we would be together one day.' Hillary's voice was icy now.

'For a time I believed I could do it....' Nicky's voice trailed away into sobs

'Well,' said Hillary, 'I don't see that there's much more to say. Guess this is goodbye.'

'Hillary, please don't go like this.'

'Say "goodbye" Nicky.'

'Hillary, please!'

'Goodbye, Nicky.' Hillary switched the phone off and put it back on its cradle.

CHAPTER 8

Nicky sat on the veranda, a cup of strong black coffee in her hand. She looked out over the garden. The rose bushes were all in flower; the apple trees in blossom. Everything looked beautiful and innocent. Even the birds were singing. Nicky had known this day would come. She had known it for almost two years. She had known how much it was going to hurt. She had drunk a dangerous amount of vodka over the past three days. Her skin felt dry and flaky and her face ached from the endless lines of coke she had done which had kept her up all night. It was Sunday morning now. Jack would be getting up soon and suggesting a walk to go and get the papers. Nicky wondered if she would ever get a good night's sleep again.

Up until a few days ago Hillary had worshipped her, loved her, and trusted her. And now Hillary knew her for what she really was; a fraud, a liar, and a cokehead. There was plenty that Hillary didn't even know yet, and would now never know. That Hillary did not work on Thursdays and Fridays at the large hardware store. Jack owned the store and a restaurant too. Nicky had been involved in the early days but she didn't need to work and had long since stopped going in. She had told Hillary that she worked because she had to explain where her income came from. Thursday and Friday were coke nights, along with Saturday and

Sunday. Saying she was tired from work had been a good excuse to explain her absences to Hillary.

Nicky and Jack did often go out at the weekends but more and more lately it was just the two of them, sitting in the lounge doing line after line of coke with the curtains drawn. The strain of keeping her two big secrets had taken its toll on Nicky and she was a lot more introverted now than she had been two years ago. Jack had noticed the change in her and complained that she was becoming lethargic and disinterested in life. He had also complained that she spent too many nights up late on the computer and then couldn't get up in the morning. But he was an easy-going man and didn't give her a hard time about it. For both of them the coke had begun to take over their lives. For Nicky it brought the numbness and nothingness that she craved. An escape from the madness of what she was doing. Even though she knew the coke in itself was madness. She had let a woman fall in love with her, made her believe that they would be together one day when all the time she knew deep down that she could never leave Jack.

She had been eleven years old when she first met Jack. Nicky went to a private catholic school for girls and Jack, who was the same age as her went to the equivalent boy's school across the road. He was a shy boy, bullied for being slightly overweight and severely dyslexic. They had begun by playing football in the park together. Nicky was a tomboy and loved her soccer. Then playing in the park had become kissing in the park and they became a teen-couple, going everywhere together. Everyone knew that when you saw Nicky there you would also see Jack. They had a shared interest in motorbikes and hung around with a group of like-minded teenagers. Others referred to them as hippies or greasers. Both Nicky and Jack had long hair and wore denims and leather. The group was still friends to this day now they were around forty. They had mostly done well in the world and had shares in each other's companies. Drugs were always part of the scene. They still smoked hash and did a few other things but the main drug of choice was cocaine.

Nicky had had a big crush on her P.E teacher at school. She kept a teenage diary in which she wrote down every interaction she had with her. But lots of girls had crushes on teachers and it never occurred to her that she might be gay.

It was when she went to university that everything changed. When she met Sinead. Nicky was only in her first week when she went into the little campus shop and saw Sinead holding court behind the counter. She was slender with cropped fair hair and was telling a joke to an assembled group in a strong Northern Ireland accent. Nicky was absolutely captivated. She found excuses whenever she could to go into the little shop and the two girls quickly became friends. Sinead was older, in her third year and this was also part of the attraction. Nicky was delighted to learn that Sinead also worked behind the bar in the university. She spent every night she could in there. Soon the two were inseparable. They got a room together in the university, which meant they got to spend lots of time alone too. Sinead was a very emotional type who was always having arguments on the phone to her mother with whom she had a very bad relationship. Nicky often found herself comforting Sinead after one of these arguments and theirs had become a very physical relationship. One night in winter after they had both had a lot to drink Nicky was holding Sinead as she sobbed in her arms and suddenly they were kissing. Within minutes they were in bed together.

The next day they could barely look at each other. They went to a nearby pub and had more drinks and both confessed they had been attracted to each other from day one. They walked home in the dark hand in hand. They became lovers. Nicky was nineteen years old.

Jack continued to visit Nicky at university, as did Sinead's boyfriend Rob. It never occurred to either girl to end their relationships with their boyfriends and come out. The year was 1980. What they had between them and what they did together when they were alone was simply a secret.

Then, after a year Nicky was thrown out of university. It wasn't surprising, as she had done very little work. Nicky's father had lost all his money and her parents had moved into a flat. Imogen had left home and got married. There was no room in the flat for Nicky. Jack had got a good job and was renting a flat of his own. He asked Nicky to move in. She loved Jack as a friend but not in the way she loved Sinead. However it was an easy solution to the housing problem she was now faced with. She moved in. It was easier to move in than not.

Sinead graduated and got a job as a social worker in Liverpool, which was where the university was. The two girls continued to visit each other. Nicky never thought of it as an affair even though she and Sinead were still lovers. Nicky knew by now that she was gay.

She didn't like sleeping with Jack and only did so when his protestations became overwhelming. But she never saw it as an option to live with Sinead as an openly lesbian couple. She saw her lesbianism as deviant behaviour, which she had to hide. She and Jack had fallen together as a couple as an act of convenience. Or at least that's how it had been for her. As for Jack, he was a one-woman man. Nicky was the only girlfriend he had ever had.

After moving in with Jack, Nicky got herself a job working in the office for a clothing importer. She and Sinead saw less and less of each other and the relationship petered out, although Nicky often thought of her. Over the twenty years she had lived with Jack, Nicky had had five more flings with various women. It wasn't hard to keep them secret, as none of the women she dated were particularly butch. She simply passed them off as friends. However she thought Jack might have been suspicious of the last one, Sarah, who was very much younger than she.

Two years had passed since the end of the affair with Sarah when Nicky had entered the gay chat room where she had met Hillary. Her lesbianism would not go away. It niggled and niggled at her like a thorn under her skin. She longed to be with a woman again and dreaded the idea of being with Jack for the rest of her life without ever feeling love again.

On the internet she had found it easy to invent a new life for herself, one where she was single and independent. A genuine, signed up, card carrying member of the gay community. She had talked to a few women before she met Hillary. With one of them she had even progressed to the phone calling stage. Most of them were married women trapped in lives with husbands they did not love in the true sense. My God! It was endemic! Just how many closet lesbians were there out there? Nicky liked the way these women looked up to her as someone who had been there and worn the T-shirt. It was a harmless lie. The internet was just a form of entertainment.

When Hillary had confided in her that first August night nearly two years ago that she was married, Nicky had liked the way the other woman had admired her for being brave enough to live her true life. Nicky had fallen in love with Hillary very quickly. It was the first time she had been in love since Sinead. The other five women over the years had been just flings. After she had got closer to Hillary, Nicky knew it was time to spill the beans. But every time she was about to tell the truth something stopped her. She didn't want to hear the disappointment in Hillary's voice. There was another reason too. Another woman in the chat room had been interested in Hillary. But she was married and Hillary had told Nicky she would never dream of getting involved with someone married. 'My own situation is difficult enough,' she had said. 'I'm looking for a single girl.' And there the mistake was made. Nicky had been living in a dream world for nearly two years in which she was that single girl that Hillary dreamed of. Whenever reality gave her a nudge the coke took care of it.

Nicky sipped her coffee. At least one of her immediate problems had been solved. She and Jack were going on holiday to Canada on Thursday for a week. She had been wondering what excuse to give to Hillary to explain another week's absence. Now she didn't have to worry about it. Imogen was going to look after the dog. Imogen of course had no idea that her sister was a lesbian, although there was no doubt she would have been horrified if she found out. Imogen was openly homophobic.

Jack came out onto the patio and sat on the step next to Nicky.

'You've been at it a bit heavily this weekend,' he said. 'Got a hangover?'

'Jack,' said Nicky. 'I want us to stop the coke. It's taken over our lives.'

*

The plane took off from Heathrow Airport at eight in the morning. Jack was asleep even before it had levelled out. He always slept on plane journeys, even car journeys. Nicky sat beside him engulfed by sadness. She hadn't done any coke since the weekend and neither had Jack to her knowledge. They had spoken about stopping many times before. In fact they had stopped for months at a time before. Jack had agreed with her that they were taking too much lately and they had said they would help each other stay off it. This week shouldn't be too difficult from that point of view as they were in new surroundings. Nicky really meant it this time that she was stopping for good. She was doing it for Hillary.

The hotel was plush and elegant. Jack had a couple of vodkas and lay down on the bed and fell asleep again. Nicky went down to the bar and ordered herself a vodka. She sat in one of the large armchairs and watched people come and go. She imagined she was here with Hillary. Hillary would find this hotel too ostentatious and that would make her unable to relax. She thought about the curtain ties and a sad little smile came over her face. She would live a comfortable life with Jack as long as she stayed with him. There would always be money for expensive holidays like this. And yet here she was in one of the most impressive hotels in Canada wishing she was in Ballybay with Hillary.

Nicky wondered just how Hillary was coping. She hadn't been coping with life at all well in the few weeks leading up to Nicky's revelations. She had told Nicky that she had lost weight, couldn't sleep and that the strain of living with Dermot and keeping her secret was wearing her down. She had also said how much she missed Nicky. It was now six months since they had seen each other. Hillary had viewed it as six wasted months of her life. The trouble was that Hillary had been unable to carry on a normal life the way Nicky had. She gave a wry smile. As if the life of a coke addict was normal.

Nicky loved Jack in a way that Hillary didn't love Dermot. Dermot wasn't good to Hillary the way Jack was to her. Jack had always been good to her and let her do whatever it was in life that made her happy. How could she repay him by leaving him?

She took another sip of vodka. It troubled her that Hillary had no real friends to console her. She had Peter and Isabel in England, but they were too far away. She had Phil but Hillary wasn't out to him yet. Nicky guessed that she would confide in her internet buddy Jemm, who, living in Australia could hardly have been further away. Hillary had no one to hug her and console her. God, Nicky felt despicable for what she had done. She went to the bar and ordered another vodka.

She sat down again and flicked through the hotel brochure on the table. Two words leapt out at her. *Internet access.* Within five minutes she had located the hotel computers and was sitting in front of one, her vodka beside her. She logged onto the internet and opened her mailbox. 'Inbox 1' it said. With shaking hands she opened the mail. It was a message from a credit card company. Her heart sank. She clicked on 'Compose' and stared at the blank page in front of her. What did she want to say?

'Dear Hillary, I still love you but I can't leave Jack so please agree to be my mistress so we can carry on as before.' She sighed. How the hell was she going to say this? She typed Hillary's e-mail address at the top and for the title she typed 'Thursday Night.' She tabbed down to the main body of the e-mail.

'Dearest Hillary,' she typed. 'I am in Canada with Jack on Holiday. I miss you like crazy and pray that you are okay.' She read it back to herself. My God it sounded terrible. Totally heartless. That she had just swaned off on holiday having delivered Hillary the cruellest of blows. Damn it she was going to have to tell another lie. She hit the delete button and began again.

Dearest Hillary,

I am in rehab and haven't taken any drugs since last Friday night. It's going to be a long hard road but they tell me admitting you have a problem is the first step.

'Wait a minute' she thought. 'They wouldn't have internet access in rehab.' She began typing again.

They have allowed me to send this to you after I explained everything. I want you to know I am alright, although I miss you like crazy. I pray that you are okay. Believe me, if there was any way I could undo what I have done to you I would. I know you must be feeling terrible right now and probably hate the sight of me. But I still love you, Hillary and hope and pray that you will remain my friend. I don't know how and I don't know when but someday we will be together. My first step is to get clean and stay clean. I am determined about this and promise I won't let you down. I'm doing this for you. I love you,

Nicky x x x

*

Jack's *Mercedes* pulled out of Nicky's drive and sped off to work. At one time, Nicky would have got up and ironed a shirt for him. But these days he had to get up and iron his own. The holiday in Canada had been a melancholy one for Nicky. She had not received a reply to her e-mail. Nicky had sneaked down to check her mail twice a day. Jack would have thought her crazy if he had seen her on the computer so much on holiday. Nicky could find no incentive to get out of bed.

That evening Nicky's friend Linda called and asked her to come down to the pub for a few drinks.

'I hardly see you these days. Come and tell me all about the Canada holiday.'

Nicky couldn't think of an excuse not to go, even though she wasn't in the mood. She got into Linda's car and they drove off.

'So,' said Linda when they were settled in the corner. 'Tell me all about the holiday.' Nicky had a pint of *Guinness* and Linda had a spritzer. Suddenly, without warning Nicky's eyes filled with tears.

'Nicky, what is it? What's wrong?' said Linda, her face full of concern.

Nicky had told nobody that she was gay. All her friends knew was that Nicky had a friend in Ireland called Hillary whom she went over to visit. All of a sudden the burden became too much to bear. A tear landed with a splash on Nicky's hand. Her dark hair fell over her face as she bowed her head.

'My friend in Ireland, Hillary. She's my girlfriend. I'm gay.'

'I had guessed that,' said Linda to Nicky's surprise, 'but what has you so upset?'

'Well I've been seeing her now for two years and she's just found out about Jack. I had told her I was single. And she's really in a state about it. She thought we were going to be living together soon.' The tears were flowing now. 'She's also just found out that I have a coke habit.'

'That I didn't know,' said Linda. 'How bad is it?'

'I've stopped now,' cried Nicky, 'but she's so disappointed in me. I'm not who she thought I was. She's not answering my e-mails and she has a horrible life with a violent husband. I'm so worried about her. I just want to look after her but I can't bring myself to leave Jack. It's all such a mess.'

'Do you love her?' asked Linda quietly.

'With all my heart.'
'Then don't lose her,' said Linda.

CHAPTER 9

Three months had passed. It was August again and Nicky's fortieth birthday. She hadn't touched drugs in all that time. Nor had she heard from Hillary. Nicky had a tax problem she had to sort out. She owed in excess of six thousand pounds. But she had twenty thousand pounds owing to her in dividends from a share she had in one of Jack's companies. The sooner that dividend was paid the sooner she would be a free woman. She would have her taxes all paid and have fourteen thousand left over to herself. Jack had always said she could keep this money once she had paid her taxes. She asked Jack when the dividend would be paid and he said Christmas. She had another four months to wait.

*

Nicky's dividend came on February the seventh. Christmas had passed by in a blur. They had spent it with Imogen, Bob and the children. Nicky had thought of her promise to Hillary about the next Christmas dinner she had. She hadn't heard from Hillary in nine months now. She had sent e-mails about once a month telling Hillary she was still clean but more than that she did not promise. But the truth was she had changed her mind about leaving Jack. Now she had her fourteen thousand pounds and she was ready. She had enough to support herself and Hillary for a year. She was going to Ireland. For good.

*

It was March the thirtieth. Nicky had her ferry ticket and her money in the bank. She had told Jack that she was going to spend two weeks with Hillary. Jack knew of Hillary as a friend Nicky had in Ireland. After Jack went to work that day Nicky loaded up the car with as many of her personal belongings as she could. She felt determined and calm. The worst part was saying goodbye to Bruce. Bruce was ten years old and in no fit state to travel. Besides which she could not bring herself to take Bruce away from Jack. As she drove away from her house for the last time the song playing on the radio sang 'I'm a survivor.'

The journey to the ferryport in Swansea was uneventful. Nicky drove onto the ferry with a feeling of excitement. She might have told Jack that she was leaving him for good were it not for the fact that he might have tried to prevent her taking the *Jeep*. She and Hillary needed wheels. She had booked a cabin on the ferry and she settled happily into it like a new home. Already her old life was receding at a fantastic rate. She could just picture Hillary's face when she opened the door. The thought made her smile all evening. She slept well as the ferry tossed and turned its way over the Irish Sea.

Nicky drove across the country feeling fresh and relaxed. Her excitement about seeing Hillary was at a high pitch. She barely stopped smiling the whole way. At last she passed Dermot's office. His car was outside.

It was one in the afternoon. She was only six miles from Hillary now. She parked at a little café and used the bathroom to wash her hands clean her teeth and tidy her hair. She drove confidently into Hillary's drive and knocked on the door. She had already planned what her first words would be. 'I've come for you Hillary. Run away with me.' There was no reply at Hillary's door.

*

Nicky felt vulnerable standing outside Hillary's house. She got back into the *Jeep* and drove around the corner. She sat at the wheel and thought. It should be safe to call Hillary on her mobile phone as Dermot was at work. Timber had barked when she had knocked on the door so Hillary wasn't out on a walk. Feeling bold she dialled Hillary's mobile number. It went straight to answerphone.

'Hi Hillary,' she said. 'It's me Nicky. I'm in Ireland and I'd like to see you. Ring me as soon as you get a chance.' Then she sent a text message with the same wording. The delivery report said 'pending' which meant Hillary had her phone switched off.

She thought she'd better find somewhere to stay the night and drove the four miles to the little village west of Hillary's house. There was a small hotel there and she booked in. She got settled in the small bedroom and then making sure she had her phone with her she went down to the bar. She ordered a chicken sandwich and a pot of tea. She couldn't imagine where Hillary could be. But there was nothing she could do but wait.

At seven o'clock Nicky drove back towards Hillary's house. She drove past and noted that Dermot's car was not there. Then she drove to the pub he drank in. Hillary had showed it to her on one of their previous trips. Sure enough there was Dermot's *Land Rover* outside. Was it possible that Hillary had started to go out with Dermot in the evenings? She thought briefly about going in but decided that that would be too much of a shock for Hillary. A shock she wouldn't be able to hide from Dermot. It was tantalising to think that Hillary might be inside just yards away. She drove back to the house and tried knocking on the door again even though there were no lights on in the house. There was no reply. Nicky got back into the *Jeep* and returned to the hotel.

Nicky did not sleep well that night. Her excitement about the prospect of seeing Hillary again was too strong. Things weren't going the way she planned but she would just have to be patient. She awoke the next morning with renewed hope that Hillary would be at home. After her breakfast Nicky drove to the house again. Dermot's car was not there so he must be at work. She tried knocking on the door again. Once again the only response was a bark from Timber. Now she was really worried. Had something happened to Hillary?

She continued to visit the house periodically for the rest of that day, and once again at night having established Dermot was in the pub. Still no response.

Now sitting in her hotel bedroom with pink walls she sat on the bed and tried to think of what to do. She had tried Hillary's phone again and it was still switched off. The message report had come through as 'message failed.' She knew what she was going to have to do although it scared her to think of it. The most important thing was to find Hillary no matter what.

*

It was early in the morning of Nicky's third day in Ireland. Trembling within she drove to Hillary's house. There was the car sitting in the drive. She went up to the front door and knocked. A fat man with iron-grey hair and a stern face answered the door.

'Hi,' said Nicky in a voice sounding more confident than she felt. 'You must be Dermot. Is Hillary at home?'

'No,' said Dermot in a surly voice. 'Who are you?'

Nicky took a deep breath. 'I'm Anne,' she said. 'I used to go to school with Hillary. I've come over on a surprise visit. When will Hillary be back?'

Dermot looked hard at her. 'She won't be coming back. She's gone.' And with that he shut the door in Nicky's face.

Nicky was stunned. She got back into the *Jeep* and reversed out of the drive. Her heart was thumping and her face ashen. Somehow she got back to her hotel. She went straight to her room, locked the door and began to cry tears of shock. 'Oh God, please help me find Hillary,' she said out loud.

CHAPTER 10

Hillary was in a deep sleep when the nurse came to wake her up.

'Time for breakfast, Hillary!' she said in a cheery voice. Hillary tried hard to stir herself. She sat on the edge of the bed while the nurse pulled the curtains from round her bed. The woman in the bed opposite was still asleep. Hillary stood up and began heading down the long corridor to the dining room. When she got there the doors were locked and a small queue had formed. The canteen worker opened the door from the inside and everyone filed in. Hillary went up to the counter and collected a bowl of *Cornflakes* and a plate of toast. She tried to find an empty table but within minutes the room filled up and soon there were eight people at the small round table. The man next to Hillary lifted the big heavy teapot and began to pour himself a cup of tea. His hands shook violently and the tea went all over the saucer. Hillary took the teapot next and poured herself a cup. She was uncomfortable sitting so close to this number of people and she tried to eat quickly. She had just got back to her bed when a nurse came round clapping her hands.

'Come on everyone, time for exercises!' she shouted. Hillary sighed and got up again.

*

It was seven o'clock. Nicky was eating steak and chips in the bar of the small hotel. She had decided what she must do and now felt dedicated to her task. After dinner she went up to her room got her jacket and keys and went out to her *Jeep*. She headed for the pub where Dermot drank.

She parked outside next to Dermot's *Land Rover*. There were only a handful of cars outside. She went in. The pub was quite dark inside. There were tiles on the floor rather than carpet. The bar was long and thin. There was no lounge. Dermot sat on his own at the bar with a pint of *Guinness*. He was talking to the barman. Nicky walked boldly up and sat on a barstool next to Dermot and asked for a pint of *Guinness*. Dermot looked at her then looked away. Nicky paid for her drink then turned to Dermot.

'I need to talk to you about Hillary,' she said.

'I told you. She's gone.'

'I'm a friend of hers and I need to know she's okay. Where has she gone?'

Dermot turned to look at her. 'She cracked up. She's in the loony bin,' he said laconically

Nicky felt her legs go weak but she fought to hold it together. She needed to find out the name of the hospital.

'What is the name of it, Dermot? I would like to go and visit her.'

There was a pause. Dermot gazed at her for several seconds. 'St Helen's Hospital in Castletown. Now quit following me around.'

'Thank you,' said Nicky tightly. 'I'm sorry I bothered you.' She got up and left leaving her pint on the table, untouched.

Nicky grabbed the map as soon as she opened the car door and quickly located Castletown. It was about fifty miles away. She drove to her hotel, collected her things and paid her bill. It was eight o'clock when she set off. The thought of poor Hillary in a psychiatric hospital was almost too much to bear. Nicky had never been into one but she imagined it to be a grim place. The drive was long and arduous, winding through a mountain pass. It was not easy in the dark. She needed all her powers of concentration to stay on the road. At last she came into the suburbs of Castletown, and finally into the town itself. She went into a tobacconist and asked directions to St Helen's.

Nicky drove up the long drive, which was lined with daffodils. The red brick building loomed large and imposing at the end of the drive. There were not many cars in the carpark. With her heart in her mouth Nicky knocked on the door of the main reception area which had a little light over it.

'Ah hello, I wonder if you can help me,' she said to a woman in a white nurse's uniform. 'I'm a friend of one of your patients, Hillary Walsh. I know it's very late but I've just come over from England and only just now found out she is here. Would it be at all possible to see her?'

'I'm afraid it's much too late for that. No visitors are allowed after eight at night,' said the nurse.

Nicky bit her nails. 'Yes I understand,' she said finally. 'What is the earliest I could come in the morning?'

'Well, Visitors are encouraged to come mainly in the evenings. But for a first visit you may come any time after ten in the morning.' The nurse had a pleasant soft face.

'Is there any chance you could tell me how she is?' Nicky asked. The nurse was a kind lady and could see genuine concern on Nicky's face.

'Well,' she began, 'it's not normal practice. If you are a close friend it's possible you may be able to speak to her doctor sometime tomorrow.'

Suddenly Nicky turned and saw a small thin woman in red tartan pyjamas who had just appeared hovering at the end of the long corridor.

'Hillary!' Nicky shouted before she could stop herself. Hillary looked down the corridor, froze for a second and then began to walk quickly down the corridor, her bare feet breaking into a run. Hillary threw herself into Nicky's arms.

'Nicky,' she said as she held her tightly. The nurse looked on smiling. Nicky felt so complete with Hillary's warm body in her arms. Both women were crying now.

Nicky held her away at arm's length so she could look into Hillary's face.

'Everything's going to be alright now Hillary, I'm going to book into a hotel in Castletown and they said I can come and see you at ten o'clock tomorrow. I'll get you out of here, and I'll visit you everyday till I do.'

'But how did you come to be here? How did you know where I was?'

'I'll explain all that tomorrow.' She hugged Hillary tightly again. 'I've come for you, Hillary. I've left Jack for good.'

Hillary's smile was broad through her tears.

'I can't believe this is happening,' she said. Nicky glanced at the nurse who raised her eyebrows as if to say, 'You'd better go now.'

'You just get a good night's sleep tonight and I'll be here at ten o'clock.' They kissed in spite of the nurse who then unlocked the door to let Nicky out. The two women clasped hands until the last moment. Nicky walked out to her *Jeep* her whole body tingling with happiness at having held Hillary again. As she turned round she saw Hillary standing waving through the glass door, the nurse's hand on her shoulder.

*

'Are you alright?' the nurse asked Hillary as the lights of Nicky's *Jeep* disappeared.

'Yes I'm really happy,' said Hillary wiping her eyes. 'That was my girlfriend, Nicky. I haven't seen her for ages.'

'Well I'm happy for you,' said the nurse. 'What were you doing wandering around at this time of night anyway?'

'I was looking for the smoking room. I have a terrible sense of direction. I just can't seem to get all these different corridors sorted out in my mind.'

'Well it's only ten minutes to meds time so you'd better hurry up,' said the nurse.

'Turn left at the end of the corridor and left again.' Hillary hurried up the corridor, scarcely believing what had just happened. She met her friend Claire who occupied the bed opposite hers as she turned the corner.

'Want to come for a quick ciggie with me?' she asked Claire.

'Sure,' said Claire. 'We've just got time before meds time.' The two women walked together. The corridor was painted faded pink with the paint peeling all over. In places there was graffiti on the wall.

Claire had slippers on. Hillary was in bare feet. The smoking room had originally been yellow but the walls were now coated nicotine brown. There was no one in when they entered but the air was thick with the smoke of the previous occupant.

They sat on the plastic orange chairs and lit up. Claire's hands shook as she lit her cigarette. Most of the residents had shaky hands. Hillary assumed it was the medication. She guessed she was on a weaker dose than most because her hands were okay.

'You'll never guess what just happened,' said Hillary.

'Hey, are you okay?' exclaimed Claire looking at her. 'You've been crying!'

'Yes. They were tears of happiness. I was just trying to sneak into the lobby for a cigarette and I heard voices down the corridor. When I looked, my girlfriend was standing there talking to the nurse.'

'But I thought you said she lived in England,' said Claire.

'She says she's left for good. She came to find me. She's going to get me out of here.'

Claire broke into a huge smile. 'Ah, I'm so happy for you Hillary,' she said giving her a little hug.

They hurried back to their ward to collect bottles of water and joined the meds queue. Some women were so heavily medicated they were swaying. Others

110

muttered to themselves. Another woman kept up a loud monologue, which she did everywhere she went. Hillary swallowed her tablet and with the distaste and discomfort she always felt she showed her open mouth to the nurses to prove she had swallowed it. She went back to her bed and rummaged in her locker for her mobile phone. Martina, the girl who occupied the bed behind Hillary's was twirling in front of the mirror repeating the phrase 'You are the most beautiful woman in Ireland.' Martina was the only patient in her ward she was frightened of. In the time she had been there she had found out that all four of the girls she shared a ward with were there because they had attempted suicide. Except for Martina they all seemed extremely depressed rather than mentally ill.

Hillary drew the curtains around herself and switched on her mobile phone. *I love you so much*, she texted. *Thank you for coming to get me.* She checked that her phone was switched to silent mode before sending it to Nicky.

I love you too, so very very much, read the text that came in reply. *You get a good night's sleep and everything will be okay. See you at ten.* Hillary switched her phone off and put it back in her locker. Already the lady with the hot milk trolley was calling them. She slipped through her curtains and collected a mug of hot milk and brought it back into her little cocoon. She sipped the milk sitting on her bed with her knees pulled up to her chest. One of the nurses put her head through the curtains and came in.

'Hi Hillary,' she said in that loud, rather patronising voice all the nurses seemed to use. 'I hear you had a late night visitor.'

'Yes,' replied Hillary, hating the way everyone else in the ward could hear every conversation through the curtains. There was absolutely no privacy in here anywhere. 'It was my girlfriend. She's just come over from England.'

'And were you happy to see her, Hillary?' said the nurse loudly sitting down on the bed too close for Hillary's comfort.

'Yes, I can't believe she's here. She didn't know I was in here.'

'And she's coming to see you in the morning, Hillary? Aren't you the lucky girl!'

Hillary fought the urge to laugh. The nurses always talked to you as if you were a child whilst gazing intently into your eyes.

'Well you just get a good night's sleep, Hillary and you'll be fresh for your visitor. Alright?' The nurse withdrew and Hillary lay on top of her bed with her eyes closed. She still could hardly believe Nicky was only a mile away in a hotel in Castletown. Martina had finished her milk and Hillary could see her feet beneath the curtain as she twirled around the room praising her own beauty again. Somehow it didn't bother her tonight. She felt sorry for all of the people in her ward tonight. They didn't have Nicky coming for them.

*

It was nine thirty. Nicky had just enjoyed a very hearty breakfast in the hotel dining room. She was showered and wearing fresh clothes. Last night she had said a prayer of thanks for Dermot. None of this would be happening now if Dermot had not told Nicky where Hillary was. Taking a last bite of toast, Nicky stood up and headed out to her *Jeep*.

In the hospital Hillary had asked the nurse if she could wear her clothes today. All the patients had access to the hospital grounds which were not secure, for this was a hospital for the mildly mentally ill, a sort of assessment centre. The serious cases were sent to St Anne's across the road. A kind of security guard made sure no one wandered off, and most were made to wear nightwear at all times to make escape more difficult. The nurse said Hillary could wear her clothes just for today. After breakfast Hillary had showered and dressed excitedly. She was allowed to miss her exercise class because she had a special visitor. When Nicky's *Jeep* arrived Hillary was standing looking through the glass windows of the lobby watching with a big smile on her face.

When Nicky came in, a nurse greeted her and said she would like a word later. Hillary hugged Nicky tightly and suggested they go and sit on a bench outside.

'Have you got a jacket in here with you?' asked Nicky. 'It's cold out there.'

'It's in my locker,' said Hillary. 'I'll show you my ward. They walked the long corridors together, passing a man who drooled and moaned.

'He's one of the worst,' said Hillary, 'a lot of them you wouldn't know there was anything wrong with them.'

Martina was the only one in the ward. She was dancing and singing. Hillary put her jacket on and they walked back to the lobby and outside.

They sat on a bench and both lit a cigarette. 'What's your hotel like?' asked Hillary.

'A lot nicer than yours,' Nicky grinned.

'So how did you come to leave Jack? I can hardly believe you are really here for good.'

'I decided a few months ago that I was ready to do it,' said Nicky. 'I just had to sort out all my taxes and things. I've got enough money to keep us for a year.'

'That's amazing, well done,' said Hillary. 'This is like Christmas.'

'I found out you were here from Dermot. He wasn't keen to tell me at first.'

'He's pretty much washed his hands of me,' said Hillary looking straight ahead.

'How come you ended up here?' asked Nicky gently, taking Hillary's hand. 'I mean, I know it was probably my fault. But how did it all come to a head?'

'Well,' said Hillary, 'I wasn't coping too well. I was crying all the time. I just couldn't cope with life without you in it. I lost all this weight. I'm only seven stone. The doctors thought I had an eating disorder when I came in. I was drinking heavily, and towards the end I became paranoid. They tell me I have had a nervous breakdown. They do blood tests all the time. They say I'm quite severely depressed. I've been on tablets since I came in here. They seem to be working because I don't cry any more.'

'Oh Hillary, I'm so sorry. This is all my fault,' said Nicky squeezing Hillary's hand.

114

'All that matters is that you are here now,' said Hillary.

'How long have you been in here?' asked Nicky.

'A month, but it feels like a year.'

'Well the first thing we need to do is to try and get you out of here.'

'They know all about you,' said Hillary. 'I guess you'll have to convince them I'll be coming out to a stable environment.'

'Well now I've found you I have to find us someplace to live. I'll get started today by buying the local paper.'

A nurse came out. 'Hello Hillary,' she said loudly. 'Are you enjoying your visit?'

'Yes thanks,' said Hillary.

'Nicky, Hillary's doctor is here and would like a word with you if you don't mind.'

'Yes, of course,' said Nicky getting up.

'I'll be fine sitting here,' said Hillary.

*

'Your girlfriend has made great progress since she first arrived here,' said the lady doctor to Nicky. Nicky tried to get comfortable on the plastic chair.

'What exactly is wrong with her?' she asked, wishing she could light a cigarette.

'She has suffered what used to be called a nervous breakdown. A depression induced psychosis. She has been depressed for a very long time and her coping mechanism finally failed, leading to a temporary psychosis which has been controlled by the drugs she is on. She was in a highly nervous and stressed state of mind. The drug is intended to smooth out her moods and she has responded very well. She also has what we call an over-emotional personality. But her moods have levelled out now. She is really ready to be released once we can be sure she is going out to a stable environment. Her husband hasn't visited her since she has been here and that relationship seems to be over. She has talked about you in depth and the nurses have told us how pleased she has been to see you. Are you planning to live with Hillary when she leaves here?'

'Yes, absolutely,' said Nicky. 'I've had problems of my own which prevented me from coming over here sooner. But I'm here to stay now and I have every intention of looking after her. I will be looking for a house to rent for us today.'

'Well, what I would suggest is that you try to visit her as much as possible over the next fortnight and we will monitor how she gets on. But I see no reason why she can't leave at the end of that period and attend on an outpatient basis.'

Hillary was sitting on the bench smiling when Nicky came out.

'Great news,' said Nicky, 'they say you might be out in two weeks.'

'That's fantastic!' cried Hillary. 'It looks like everything is going our way at last.'

*

Nicky had looked at three houses now, all of which were in a very bad state of disrepair. Two of them smelled of damp. Now she was driving towards the little village of Killbrack. The advert was circled in the newspaper on the passenger seat beside her. The house, when she reached it, was a beautiful white cottage standing on its own. It had a view of a lake on its east side and to the west was a forest of pine trees, and beyond that, purple mountains. The landlady showed her around inside. Nicky's favourite room was the bedroom. It had white thick walls and blue bed coverings. The window faced the lake. The lounge was small with a cosy looking open fire. The kitchen was a pretty room with latticed windows.

'I'll take it,' said Nicky.

At six o'clock Nicky arrived back at St Helen's. There was no sign of Hillary in the lobby so she walked the long corridors till she came to Hillary's ward. The curtains were open and Hillary was asleep on the bed. Nicky pulled a chair up and Hillary opened her eyes.

'Hello. What a lovely surprise! It's great to see you. I must have fallen asleep.'

'Hey, you've got your day clothes on,' said Nicky.

'Yes,' said Hillary, sitting up. 'I asked them if I could wear them and they said I could. I saw the doctor today. She says they would be happier if I joined in more. They think I'm too withdrawn. I tried to tell them that I'm a naturally quiet person, but the doctor says I should try to go to some of the classes. So I've been a good little patient today. I've been to occupational therapy and the beauty class.'

'You! In a beauty class?'

'I know,' giggled Hillary. 'I had a job escaping having make up put on me!'

'How are you feeling?' asked Nicky.

'A bit groggy at times but I'm just so happy now that you are here.'

'Guess what I've been doing today?'

'What?'

'Moving into our new house.'

'Oh!' Hillary's eyes shone; her smile lighting up her whole face. 'You've found somewhere? That's wonderful, Nicky.' They held hands as Nicky described the cottage in detail. A little tear of happiness ran down Hillary's cheek. Nicky brushed it away.

'It's just perfect,' said Nicky gently. 'All that's missing is you.'

*

It was the Thursday before Easter. Hillary had just been signed out of the hospital by her doctor. She had sent a text to Nicky to say she was ready. Now she sat in the lobby with Claire, her rucksack on her knee.

'I'll come and visit you,' she said to Claire.

'God, anyone would think you would want to see the back of this place forever,' said Claire.

'I never want to be a patient in here again, but I'd imagine it's a lot easier coming through those doors when you know you will be let out again in an hour.'

'You just get back to your cottage with Nicky and have a happy life. You're a lucky girl. She really loves you, I can tell.'

'I know,' said Hillary.

*

118

Nicky put the flowers in a vase, filled it with water and set it on the kitchen table. There was a banner up saying 'Welcome Home'. She put the champagne in the fridge. Everything was ready. She smoothed her jumper down and climbed into the *Jeep*.

Nicky turned into the entrance to St Helen's and drove up the drive for the last time. The masses of daffodils lining the long drive spoke of promise and new beginnings. She parked and saw Nicky and Claire coming out of the building. Claire was in a nightdress and dressing gown. Hillary looked frail and beautiful.

'I'll miss you. I'll see you soon,' said Hillary hugging Claire.

'You take care now. Goodbye.'

Hillary climbed into the *Jeep*. 'You've cleaned it,' she said.

'Only the best transport for my girl,' said Nicky.

'Now I really am your girl, aren't I?'

'You are mine forever, Hillary,' said Nicky taking her hand. 'And I'm taking you home.'

'Why are we taking this road?' asked Hillary as they turned left out of the hospital grounds.

'Well I kind of hoped you fancied a long drive because we have one last job to do,' said Nicky.

'What's that?' said Hillary.

'To fetch Timber, of course.'

THE END

Contact Rain McAlistair at:

rainmcalistair@eircom.net

Made in the USA
Lexington, KY
17 May 2011